DRAGON
and THIEF

Don't get left behind!

STARSCAPE
Let the journey begin . . .

From the Two Rivers
The Eye of the World: Part 1
by Robert Jordan

To the Blight
The Eye of the World: Part 2
by Robert Jordan

Ender's Game
by Orson Scott Card

The Cockatrice Boys
by Joan Aiken

Mairelon the Magician
by Patricia C. Wrede

Ender's Shadow
by Orson Scott Card

The Whispering Mountain
by Joan Aiken

Orvis
by H. M. Hoover

The Garden Behind the Moon
by Howard Pyle

The Dark Side of Nowhere
by Neal Shusterman

Prince Ombra
by Roderick MacLeish

The Magician's Ward
by Patricia C. Wrede

A College of Magics
by Caroline Stevermer

Deep Secret
by Diana Wynne Jones

Pinocchio
by Carlo Collodi

Another Heaven,
Another Earth
by H. M. Hoover

Hidden Talents
by David Lubar

The Wonder Clock
by Howard Pyle

Obernewtyn
by Isobelle Carmody

The Shadow Guests
by Joan Aiken

This Time of Darkness
by H. M. Hoover

Song in the Silence
by Elizabeth Kerner

Red Unicorn
by Tanith Lee

Putting Up Roots
by Charles Sheffield

The Billion Dollar Boy
by Charles Sheffield

In the Land of the
Lawn Weenies
by David Lubar

The Farseekers
by Isobelle Carmody

Starswarm
by Jerry Pournells

A School for Sorcery
by E. Rose Sabin

The Eye of the Heron
by Ursula K. Le Guin

Ashling
by Isobelle Carmody

The Cyborg from Earth
by Charles Sheffield

Peter Pan
by J. M. Barrie

The Hunt Begins
The Great Hunt: Part 1
by Robert Jordan

New Threads in the Pattern
The Great Hunt: Part 2
by Robert Jordan

Greyfax Grimwald
by Niel Hancock

DRAGON
and THIEF

TIMOTHY ZAHN

STARSCAPE

A TOM DOHERTY ASSOCIATES BOOK
NEW YORK

To my sister Carol,
who pointed Jack and Draycos
in the right direction

DRAGON AND THIEF: A DRAGONBACK ADVENTURE

Copyright © 2003 by Timothy Zahn

A Starscape Book
Published by Tom Doherty Associates, LLC
175 Fifth Avenue
New York, NY 10010

www.starscapebooks.com

ISBN: 0-765-34272-3

First Starscape edition: March 2004

Printed in the United States of America

0 9 8 7 6 5 4 3 2 1

CHAPTER 1

"Draycos? Come on, symby, shake a scale."

Draycos looked up from the systems monitor he'd been watching, his ears swiveling upward toward the voice. Polphir, his Shontine host, was halfway up the ladder to the *Haven-seeker*'s main navigation bubble, looking quizzically down at him. "Come on where?" Draycos called back. "We're here. We've arrived. Our job is over."

"Hardly, my good but lazy K'da," Polphir said dryly. "All the long-range navigation may be finished, but we still have to double-check the location of that planet down there. Come on, let's go."

"Very well, my good but slave-driving Shontin," Draycos replied. Crouching low, gathering all four paws under him, he leaped over the bank of monitors—and, incidentally, the two Shontine working at them—and landed precisely at the foot of the ladder. He would have preferred to jump directly to the navigation bubble and skip the climb entirely, but there was another K'da crouched at the monitor station on the lower bubble deck, and there wasn't enough room for Draycos to land there without bowling her over. Wrapping his paws around the ladder's side rails—only the Shontine used the ladder's rungs—he started up.

The *Havenseeker* was alive with activity and quiet commotion today. Small wonder: after nearly two years in space, the four bulky ships of the Shontine/K'da advance team had finally reached their goal, the world known as Iota Klestis, and everyone aboard was excited. Several times as Draycos made his way upward, one or the other of his pointed ears twitched around as an odd noise or fragment of conversation caught his attention.

Polphir was already in his seat at the wraparound control board, working busily, when Draycos reached the bubble. For a moment he paused at the top of the ladder, gazing out at the blue-green planet turning slowly beneath them. An uninhabited world, or so their contacts in this region of space had assured them. Uninhabited, and unwanted. Exactly what they needed.

> *'Twas night and blackness all around:*
> *K'da and Shontine held their ground . . .*

"You just going to sit there and daydream?" Polphir called over his shoulder. "Or were you taking a moment to admire yourself?"

"And why not?" Draycos countered, arching his long neck as he pretended to pose. "Have you ever seen a more handsome representative of the K'da people?"

"If you think I'm going to answer a question like that in here, you're crazy," Polphir told him, his voice rippling with good humor. "Wait till we get down to the planet where I've got room to duck, then ask me again."

"Never mind," Draycos said. In truth, he hadn't even noticed his reflection in the smoothly curved plastic of the bubble until Polphir made his comment. Now, though, he took a moment to focus on the image.

It wasn't a bad face, really, he decided. The long, triangular head was mostly proportioned right, the glowing green eyes beneath the bony protective ridges properly spaced. The spiny crest extending from between the eyes over the top of his head and down his long back was just about right, though perhaps a bit too narrow. His long muzzle with its razor-sharp teeth was well shaped, though some of the teeth themselves were a little crooked and his forked tongue stuck out a little too far whenever he tasted the air. His scales were a decent enough color, bright gold with red edges, though as a child he'd secretly wished they'd been gray instead. The rest of his body wasn't visible in the reflection, but he could picture it in his mind's eye: the body long and sleek, as befit a K'da warrior, the whiplike tail a little too short as it restlessly beat the air.

After two years, he decided, it would be good to feel ground beneath his paws again. Turning to face Polphir's broad back, he crouched and leaped.

His outstretched front paws touched the Shontin's bare shoulders and flattened out, sliding along the skin in both directions along his arms. As the rest of his body reached Polphir's, each part altered from three-dimensional to two-dimensional form as it flowed onto his host's body. A split second later the transformation was complete, leaving Draycos stretched like a living tattoo across Polphir's back and legs and arms.

"Anyway, I'm not sure I'd trust you to judge K'da beauty," he added, sliding his now flat head along the skin of Polphir's shoulder and around to his chest so that he could see the indicator lights better. "And just for the record, I was neither daydreaming nor admiring myself. If you must know, I was composing an epic poem about our journey here, and the beginning of new hope for our peoples."

"Were you, now," Polphir said, working at his control board.

"Yes, indeed," Draycos assured him. He stretched his front legs out and away from Polphir's arms, the limbs becoming three-dimensional again as they left the Shontin's skin, and began punching in code on his own set of control panels. "I was going to give you a good part in it, too."

"I'm flattered," Polphir said. "Really. Okay, here we go. Can you get the anterior star-fix going?"

"Already on it."

"Thanks," Polphir said. "If I were you, though, I wouldn't go writing up this voyage as a success just yet. I notice that no one seems willing to give us a straight answer as to whether we're going to be welcome here."

Draycos lifted his head from Polphir's shoulder, letting it become three-dimensional again, for a better look at the proximity display. Was that something flicking in and out at the very edge of the nav sensor's range? "You worry too much," he said soothingly, laying his head flat against Polphir's skin again and continuing to key in his star-scan. "Why would anyone object to our using a planet no one else seems to want? Especially when we're willing to pay for it."

"There are all sorts of reasons they might object," Polphir said. "Refugees in general aren't always welcome, you know. They're even less welcome when they've got enemies as dangerous as the Valahgua."

"The Valahgua will never find us," Draycos said firmly. "Not here."

Polphir shook his head. "I hope you're right."

"Spacecraft approaching," a Shontine voice called across the control complex.

"Recognition signals," another voice put in, this one a K'da. "It's our contact."

"I would say that confirms we've got the right planet," Polphir remarked, hunching his shoulders as he stretched his arms forward over the control board.

"Seems reasonable," Draycos agreed as he again lifted his head from Polphir's skin and studied the main sensor display. "Iota Klestis," he pronounced the syllables of the planet's alien name carefully. "It has a certain rhythm to it."

"Yes, it does," Polphir said. "I still vote we rename it."

"It *is* hard to find a good rhyme for," Draycos conceded. There were four ships showing on the screen now, small and compact. "Odd. None of them matches the profile of the ship the contact has used before. At least, not according to probe team records."

"Hmm." Polphir abandoned his stretching and leaned closer to the display. "You're right. You suppose one of the local governments decided to send a welcoming committee?"

"And they offered our contact a ride?"

"Or came without him," Polphir said, his tone ominous. "Maybe this planet isn't as unwanted as we were led to believe."

"Perhaps." Draycos rumbled in the back of his throat. "Still, they *do* have the correct recognition signal."

"Point," Polphir agreed, swiveling around to a different

section of the board. "Let's see if we can get a better look at them."

The image on the screen wavered, then came back sharper and clearer. Draycos had just enough time to notice the over-sized engines and multiple weapons bubbles dotting their hulls—

And then, to his amazement, three of the bubbles on each of the ships popped open in perfect unison, and twelve missiles streaked out toward the Shontine/K'da ships.

"Alert!" someone shouted. "We're under attack!"

"All warriors, to your stations," the calmer voice of Shontine Commander Chayd cut over the sudden pandemonium from the control complex deck below. "Defensive response only. This may simply be a case of mistaken identity. Comm station, talk to them—tell them who we are."

"We *are* talking," a K'da voice insisted as the ship began to shudder with the firing of its defense missiles. "They're ignoring us."

"Watch out—they're breaking formation," Polphir warned, leaning close to stare out the bubble at the incoming ships. "They're splitting up, one for each of us."

"Batteries, free fire," Chayd ordered. "Concentrate on crippling their weapons. Maybe it's still not too late to talk some sense into them."

Polphir clicked his tongue. "I don't like this, Draycos," he said quietly. "Four of them; four of us. This isn't a chance meeting. They were waiting for us."

"If they were, they didn't get the details very clear," Draycos pointed out. "Missiles that size, against hull armor as thick as ours? What do they think they're trying to prove?"

"And once they did know what they were up against, why

split up their firepower?" Polphir added. "Why not concentrate everything on one ship at a time?"

"Or just turn and run?" Draycos said. "They're up to something, Polphir. The question is, what?"

Polphir never had a chance to reply. Instead, the ship sweeping toward them provided the answer. From a weapon bubble near its center came a sickly-yellowish flash, and a slender cone of violet light lanced out.

Draycos caught his breath, his mind refusing for that first awful second to believe what he was seeing. Here, hundreds of light-years from their beleaguered worlds, it was impossible that their enemy's most terrifying weapon should be ignited against them.

Yet there it was: the all-too-familiar cone of writhing violet light twisting its way toward the aft end of their ship. The weapon no shielding could block, and that no living being could survive.

The weapon called simply the Death.

"Evasive!" Chayd shouted. "All ships!"

But it was too late. As Draycos watched from his perch on Polphir's back and shoulders he could see that there would be no chance for any of them. All four attacking fighters had ignited the violet beams now, focusing them on the sterns of their chosen colony ships.

And over the all-ship intercom, Draycos could hear the horrified shouts, suddenly cut off, as the Shontine and K'da in the *Havenseeker*'s engine room were caught in the beam and died.

"Evasive!" the commander shouted again, his voice hard and desperate.

A second later Draycos found himself grabbing for the grip

bars at the edge of the control panel as the *Havenseeker* twisted downward out of the violet light sweeping slowly forward along the hull.

How their pilot had managed to coax a maneuver like that from such a big, lumbering ship he couldn't imagine. It was clear their attacker couldn't imagine it either, because for a few seconds the violet beam burned harmlessly through space above the ship as its target dropped out from under it. At the same time, a full salvo of missiles shot from the *Havenseeker*'s flank toward the fighter.

Draycos held his breath as the fighter twisted madly to get out of the way. It successfully evaded most of the missiles; but then the law of averages caught up with it, and the last two slammed full into its side just aft of the Death weapon.

"Two hits!" Polphir called. "The Death—"

He broke off, sagging slightly in his seat as the rest of his lungful of air escaped without words.

There was nothing else to say. Despite the torn and blackened metal on the fighter's side where the *Havenseeker*'s missiles had struck, the violet beam was still twisting its way out into space. It swiveled down toward the *Havenseeker,* still driving away on its evasive course, and settled again on the colony ship's side. Almost as if nothing had happened, the beam resumed its steady progress forward.

So too did the cries of the dying. With a shudder, Draycos reached out and shut off the nav bubble's intercom. There was nothing he could do to help the Shontine and K'da back there. Nothing anyone could do. The cries continued, more faintly, coming from the intercom speakers on the control deck below.

"This is impossible," Polphir murmured. He sounded more

bewildered than frightened. "How could the Valahgua be here? How could those ships have the Death?"

"I don't know," Draycos said. "It doesn't look like we'll have the chance to find out, either."

"No, I suppose not," Polphir said, his voice almost peaceful. A Shontin unafraid to die, and for a brief moment Draycos envied him that calm.

The *Havenseeker* was still pitching away from its attacker. But the enemy was wise to its tricks now. The violet beam remained steady, continuing its slow sweep forward. In his mind's eye, Draycos could see his companions' bodies slumped in their seats or lying crumpled on the deck as the beam snuffed out their lives and then moved on. The Shontine bodies would linger for awhile; those of the K'da, he knew, would already be turning two-dimensional and rippling away into nothingness. A K'da death left no body for his friends to mourn.

The beam was nearly to the control complex now, and Draycos could feel a slight and unpleasant electric tingle along the scales on that side. "Here it comes," he said. Oddly enough, his voice sounded almost as calm and peaceful as Polphir's had, even though he was far from feeling that way. "It's been an honor to be associated with you, Polphir—"

"Wait a moment," Polphir cut him off, leaning forward and pointing toward their attacker. "It sputtered just then—there. Did you see it?"

"Yes," Draycos said, frowning. The yellow source-glow was indeed flickering; and now so was the violet Death beam itself. Had the near-misses by the *Havenseeker*'s missiles done some damage after all?

And then, with one final flicker, both the yellow and violet lights went out.

"They've shut it off," Draycos breathed, blinking in bewilderment. Was this some kind of cruel trick? One last gasp of false hope for the few survivors here at the *Havenseeker*'s bow before their unknown enemy turned the Death on them again?

But the weapon remained off. Draycos watched, afraid to believe it, as the fighter began to pull up and away. "What are they playing at?" he wondered aloud. "Do they think they got all of us?"

"I would say they're just saving themselves a little trouble," Polphir said grimly. "Take a look. That last maneuver put us into the atmosphere."

Draycos hissed around his tongue. Polphir was right; the thin white condensation trails were smoking off the tips of the antennas rising from the hull.

Commander Chayd seemed to have become aware of their danger at the same time. "Full lateral power," he ordered sharply.

"Not responding," the pilot called back. "Control lines are out."

"Drosh, Mintuk—get to the engine room," Chayd snapped. "You'll need to operate the drive manually."

"Do you want us to go, too?" Polphir called, starting to unstrap.

"No, you two stay there," Chayd said. "Landing sensors are also out. We'll need you to guide us in visually."

Polphir glanced over his shoulder, his eyes briefly meeting Draycos's. Draycos could guess his thought: that such a feat would be nearly impossible to carry out.

But there was nothing for it but to do their best. "Yes, sir," Polphir said, resealing his restraints.

"Everyone to your stations," Chayd said. There was little hope, Draycos knew, and he had no doubt that Chayd knew it too. But the commander was a Shontine warrior, and he would never simply give up without a struggle. Not while any of his crew remained alive. "Prepare yourselves," Chayd added. "One way or another, we're going down."

CHAPTER 2

"Jack? Come on, lad, rise and shine."

"Yeah, yeah," Jack Morgan muttered, turning over in his narrow bed and pulling the covers more tightly around his thin shoulders. It felt early, and he didn't feel much like getting up.

Not much point to getting up, anyway. There was nothing to do here, not unless he wanted to sit around outside the *Essenay* and pull apart pieces of the grass outside, the stuff that reminded him of bluish-green curly fries. He'd spent part of yesterday doing that, and the thrill of it had faded mighty fast.

"Come on, lad, rise and shine," his uncle's voice came again. This time, the cabin's lights came on, too.

Jack pulled the covers up partway over his head, squeezing his eyes shut against the light and trying hard to hold onto the quick temper that had gotten him into trouble so many times on so many different worlds. Uncle Virgil had been on his case forever about that temper.

But then, Uncle Virgil had also been on his case about his lack of respect for authority, too. Which was kind of funny, considering Uncle Virgil's chosen profession.

"Come on, lad, rise and shine," Uncle Virge said again.

It was insulting, too, on top of everything else. *Rise and shine* was how you woke up a five-year-old, not someone who'd turned fourteen a full month ago. On some worlds out there you could be a soldier at age fourteen, for Petey's sake. He would bet long odds that soldiers didn't get *rise and shine* as *their* wake-up call.

"Come on, lad, rise and shine."

"Why should I?" Jack growled, trying to burrow deeper beneath his covers. "What, the cows need milking? I'm going to be late for school? What?"

"There's something outside you need to see," Uncle Virge said. "Come on, lad, rise—"

"Okay, okay, I'm up, I'm up," Jack snapped the magic words, throwing off the covers and swinging his legs over the edge of the bed as he sat up. The sudden change in altitude made his head go woozy, and he sat there rubbing his eyes until the feeling passed. "You want to maybe turn the lights down a little?"

The light obediently faded from painful to merely annoying. Cautiously, he pried open his eyelids.

The first thing in his line of sight was the display screen on the far wall of his cabin. Normally, the screen was set to show engine status or current nav data or some such ship's function. With most of the *Essenay*'s systems shut down since landing here two days ago, he had reset the screen to show the lush green Iota Klestis landscape stretching out beyond the main airlock hatchway. It was sort of like having a window in his room, though it had been so long since he'd had a normal groundside room with a normal window that he could hardly remember what it was like.

At least, the screen was supposed to show the outside view. At the moment, all it showed was black.

He turned to look at the clock built into the bulkhead beside his bed. No wonder there was nothing to see out there: the glowing numbers read 4:57 A.M. "Are you out of your shrink-wrapped mind?" he demanded. "It's five o'clock in the morning!"

"Go outside," Uncle Virge said. "There's something out there—"

"Yeah, yeah, I heard you," Jack sighed, plucking his jeans from the swing-out arm where they were hanging and pulling them on. Arguing with Uncle Virgil had never been a very rewarding pastime. Arguing with Uncle Virge was even less so. "This had better be good."

He was retrieving a set of electronic binoculars from the airlock's storage cubbyhole when Uncle Virge suddenly cut in again. "Uh-oh," he said, his voice coming now from the airlock intercom speaker. "Get outside, Jack lad. Quickly."

The hatch popped and the gangway slid out to the ground below. "Where?" Jack asked, turning on the 'nocs and peering cautiously out the hatch. He hadn't run into any serious predators since landing, but the planet was bound to have some stashed away somewhere. Was that what Uncle Virge was all worked up about?

"Not there," Uncle Virge said urgently. "Up. Go down the ramp and look up, toward the eastern horizon. Hurry."

Grimacing, Jack trudged down the ramp. If Uncle Virge had hauled him out of bed to show him some cool aurora borealis or something, he was going to take him apart molecule by molecule. Lifting the 'nocs, he focused on the sky to the east.

There were flickers of light up there, all right. But it was no aurora.

It was a space battle.

"Oh, no," Jack groaned, his heart jumping suddenly into his throat. A space battle over his nice, quiet, out-of-the-way hiding place?

"My words exactly, lad," Uncle Virge said, his voice grim. "There were only those four big ships showing when I woke you. I thought we might have stumbled in on a smugglers' rendezvous."

"Terrific," Jack muttered, adjusting the focus as best he could. Along with the four big ships were four little ones—he could barely make them out at this range, but the glowing light from their drives was easily visible. They were definitely the attackers, firing flurries of missiles as they charged the big ships.

He could see some missile trails going the other direction now. "They're starting to shoot back," Uncle Virge commented. "Seem a bit slow on the uptake."

"Maybe they weren't expecting trouble," Jack said. "You have a make on any of them?"

"Not the big ones," Uncle Virge said. "They look like long-haul freighters, but I don't recognize the design. The little ones are Djinn-90 pursuit craft. A favorite of mercenaries, planetary militaries, and dockyard police throughout the Orion Arm."

Police. Jack had gotten so he cringed even at the word. "So are you saying those *are* smugglers up there?"

"Not saying they are; not saying they aren't," Uncle Virge said. "Could be it's pirates attacking mining ships."

"You told me there weren't any mines here."

"I said there was nothing on the books on this place,"

Uncle Virge corrected. "Doesn't mean some ambitious citizen isn't doing something on the quiet. Hold on a minute—what's that?"

Jack frowned, pressing the 'nocs harder to his eyes. In exact unison, something that looked like a slender purple tornado had erupted from each of the four small ships. "Plasma bursts?" he suggested.

"If they are, it's not like anything on the books," Uncle Virge said. "Not like anything else I've ever heard of, either. Doesn't seem to be doing any damage, though."

"Better check that," Jack advised, the back of his neck feeling the strain as the ships' paths carried them higher and higher in the sky over his head. "One of them's dropping out of orbit. Either it's hurt, or else it's trying to get away."

"It might as well save itself the effort," Uncle Virge said. "A ship that size and shape maneuvers like a sleepy brick. There—you see? They've got it targeted again."

Jack nodded silently as the purple tornado caught up with the dodging freighter and began raking across it again. "You think anybody's going to notice us down here?"

"Not likely," Uncle Virge assured him. "We're not putting out any power to speak of, and I've got the chameleon hull-wrap going. Besides, this world is supposed to be uninhabited. Who'd think of looking for anyone here?"

"Right," Jack said. That was, after all, the whole reason he and the *Essenay* were on Iota Klestis in the first place.

Unless . . .

"Unless this is some kind of sneak trick," he suggested slowly. "A fake battle they're hoping will smoke us out?"

Uncle Virge gave a clearly audible snort. "You want subtlety, lad, you'd better look someplace besides Braxton Universis. Megacorporations are by definition big, slow, and obvious."

"StarForce, then?" Jack persisted. "Or Internos Police?"

"Megacorporations by a different name," Uncle Virge said. "Besides, we're talking a pretty expensive trick here. Show me *any* law enforcement agency that has that much spare cash lying around."

Jack made a face. "So it's a real battle."

Earlier, the purple tornadoes had fired out from the small ships at exactly the same time. Now, again in exact unison, they shut off again. "Well, it *was* a real battle," Uncle Virge corrected. "It may be over now. Uh-oh."

"What?"

"The ship that tried to dodge," Uncle Virge said. "Looks like it's headed for a crash landing."

Jack adjusted the range finder on his 'nocs. Uncle Virge was right; the big ship was falling. Already he could see the shock-wave distortion as it dipped ever deeper into the atmosphere. "Is it under power?"

"Limited power, yes," Uncle Virge said. "Also limited control. Doesn't look like he'll have nearly enough of either, though."

Jack squeezed the 'nocs hard, feeling sick as he watched the ship trying valiantly to maneuver. They weren't headed for any crash landing, not at that speed and angle. They were headed for a crash, period. "Nothing we can do for them, I suppose," he murmured.

"No," Uncle Virge said thoughtfully. "But maybe there's something *they* can do for *you*."

Jack lifted his eyes away from the 'nocs, throwing a sideways look at the soft light inside the airlock. That was a tone of voice he knew far too well. "Like what?"

"Like maybe after the dust settles we might find something worth salvaging from the wreck."

"Uh-*huh*."

"Oh, come on, lad, don't use that tone with me," Uncle Virge said, sounding hurt. "The ship's a goner—you can see that from here. Whatever's aboard won't do them any good, may they rest in peace."

"And so why don't we pretend we're vultures and see what we can sift out of the rubble?" Jack suggested.

"Well, if it isn't us, it'll be our friends in the Djinn-90s," Uncle Virge pointed out. "They aren't wasting any time checking out their other prizes, you know."

Frowning, Jack lifted the 'nocs again. Sure enough, the four small ships were moving into docking positions alongside the three remaining freighters.

"Still, they ought to be busy up there for quite some time." Uncle Virge's voice went all soft and silky. "And you know, if they *were* smugglers, whatever they were carrying was probably valuable. Maybe even valuable enough to pay off Braxton Universis."

Jack shook his head. "I don't want to steal anymore. You know that."

"You want to stay on the run forever?" Uncle Virge countered. "This could be a way to square things."

"I'm trying to put the past behind me," Jack insisted.

"And see where it got you," Uncle Virge shot back. "On the run for a crime you didn't even commit. You see any fairness in *that*?"

Jack sighed. "I don't see much fairness in anything anymore."

"Exactly my point," Uncle Virge said. "Besides, there's no crime in stealing stolen goods, now, is there?"

"I'm sure you and the law have different opinions on that."

"Jack, my lad," Uncle Virge said, back to that injured tone again.

"Yeah, yeah, I know," Jack said, lifting the 'nocs to his eyes again. He had to turn around to see the freighters; while he'd been arguing with Uncle Virge, they'd passed over his head on their way to the western horizon. "Even if they ignore the crash, aren't they going to spot us as soon as we take off?"

"Only if they can see us," Uncle Virge pointed out reasonably. "All we have to do is wait until they're out of sight over the horizon, then take off and head toward the crash site. Before they come back over the eastern horizon we'll go to ground and wait until they pass around the other side again. Couldn't be easier."

"How long will it take us to get there?" Jack asked.

"Three, four hours, maybe," Uncle Virge said. "Five at the most."

"And you don't think the guys in the Djinn-90s will be checking it out themselves?"

"Oh, come on, lad," Uncle Virge said. "Look at the size of those freighters. It could be days before they finish up there and turn their attention to the wreck."

Jack chewed at his lip. There was something about this that felt monumentally stupid. All his instincts were screaming at him to get the *Essenay* out of here the minute everyone's back was turned.

But if there really *was* a way to square things with Braxton Universis, maybe it was worth a try.

He shook his head bitterly. A month ago, on his fourteenth birthday, he'd baked himself a birthday cake, with little candles and everything. Uncle Virge had sung an off-key "Happy Birthday," and Jack had actually made a secret wish as he blew out the candles.

The wish had been that, after all these years, he could finally make a normal life for himself.

So much for the mystical power of wishes.

"Shall I fire up the preflight checklist?" Uncle Virge prompted.

Jack let the 'nocs fall to his side. "Sure," he said, turning and trudging back up the ramp. "Let's go take a look."

CHAPTER 3

Commander Chayd did his best, as did all the remaining Shontine and K'da. But the *Havenseeker* was too big, its control areas too widely scattered.

In the end, there really was no hope.

Draycos regained consciousness slowly, to find himself lying beneath the nav bubble's control board. He was curled up tightly with his back to the bulkhead like a K'da cub trying to keep warm on a cold night, a mound of broken tiles and shattered equipment pressed against him. The descent through the atmosphere—the heat and buffeting, the tension and Chayd's calm orders—was etched on his mind like the brilliant sunlight of morning. But the crash itself was only a vague memory of noise and chaos, of being thrown violently about as the ship's hull crumpled beneath him and the nav bubble shattered above him.

For that matter, he couldn't even remember leaving the relative safety of Polphir's back and becoming fully three-dimensional again.

He had no idea how long he'd been lying there. Long enough for what was left of the *Havenseeker* to grind its way to a halt, apparently, because all was now silence and stillness. On the other hand, the cloud of dust that still hung thick in the air around him showed that the ship hadn't been down for very long, either. An hour, perhaps. Maybe less.

Carefully, trying not to choke on the dust, he took a deep breath, concentrating on the feel of the muscles and bones in his torso as his chest expanded. There were a few aches and pains, but nothing that indicated anything more serious than bruises and a few cracked scales through which blood was slowly oozing. He tried his legs next, carefully moving and twisting each in turn. The middle joint of his left rear leg jolted him with a brief stab of pain, but after a little experimentation he concluded it was only a mild sprain. He catalogued a few more bruises and cracked scales on various limbs, then moved on to his neck and tail. Again, he found nothing serious.

Pushing away the collected debris hemming him in, he worked his way out from under the control panel. Polphir was nowhere to be seen, the chair he'd been strapped to apparently torn straight off the deck. Wincing as shards of plastic and metal crunched under his paws, Draycos walked gingerly to the edge of the bubble floor and looked down to the main deck.

There, lying amid the rubble, was Polphir.

Draycos's injured leg and the uncertain footing on the main deck would make a standard K'da leap risky at best. Fortunately, the ladder he'd climbed up earlier was still in place, though hanging precariously by a single connector. Climbing down as quickly as he could, he crunched through more plastic and metal to Polphir's side.

The Shontin was dead.

Draycos would not remember afterward how long he crouched there, sifting quietly through his memories and saying his silent farewells. He thought back to their first meeting, after Draycos's host had died, and to those first few tentative months as symbionts. He had missed Trachan terribly, and only much later did he learn that his surly attitude had nearly persuaded Polphir to turn him over to someone else instead.

But the Shontin had been patient, and Draycos had managed to grow up a little. In the end, they had worked things out.

It had been lucky for Draycos that they had. At least twice in their time together it had been only Polphir's quick thinking in the face of danger that had kept the two of them alive.

But it hadn't all been merely experience and quick thinking. Polphir had had a fierce loyalty to his symbiont, a loyalty he'd demonstrated at the Battle of Conkren when he'd deliberately put his own life on the line for his friend. Draycos still shuddered at that memory, and still marveled at the miracle that had gotten both of them out alive.

Now Polphir was gone. And Draycos had been powerless to save him.

Or even to properly mourn him. He and Polphir had been together for over ten years, as companions, symbionts, and fellow warriors. A proper farewell to such a relationship could not be accomplished in less than a week, nor without all of Polphir's close family and friends on hand to weave their own memories into the great tapestry that would close off his life.

But what remained of Polphir's close family was a long ways away. Most of his friends lay dead around him here on the *Havenseeker*'s deck.

And Draycos certainly did not have a week for a proper mourning. In fact, unless he could find another host, his own life could be counted now in hours.

"Steady, K'da warrior," he said aloud to himself. His voice was startlingly loud in the silence, the words echoing oddly from the new contours and gaps the crash had created. "Rule One: assess the complete situation before coming to unpleasant conclusions."

As a pep talk, it was a dismal failure. As good military advice, though, it made sense. Picking his way through the debris, favoring his injured leg a little, he began to search the ship.

It was an unpleasant duty. The *Havenseeker*'s bow was completely crushed and buried, the few Shontine who had been up there apparently buried with it. Those who had been below him in the control complex had also died in the crash. From the control complex aft, the ship was clogged with debris but otherwise relatively undamaged, and for awhile Draycos dared to hope that their attackers' sweep with the Death might have missed someone.

But no. They had done an efficient job of it, leaving nothing behind but Shontine bodies. Some lay where they had fallen, most where the crash had sent them sliding.

The K'da bodies, of course, were long gone.

Slowly, his head held low, Draycos turned and headed back forward to the control complex. It was, he thought more than once along the way, worse than any battlefield from which he had ever faced the Valahgua. On battlefields, at least, there were always a few survivors. Here, there was no one but him.

But he would be joining the rest of them soon enough. He had survived an attack with the Death, and even made it through a ship crash. But he could not survive for long without a host. Another two hours, perhaps, and he would fade into a two-dimensional shadow and disappear forever into nothingness.

Still, he had those two hours. He might as well put them to use.

The sensor station in the control complex had been completely demolished in the crash. But the piloting console had its own recorder, which turned out to be relatively undamaged.

The data diamonds, unfortunately, had been jolted out of their recording slots by the impact and mixed together in a random heap at the bottom of the recorder housing. Digging them out, he found a handheld reader and began sorting through them. Before death took him, perhaps he could at least learn who had done this to them.

Though even as he set to work, he knew down deep that he was merely distracting himself. Whatever he learned here, that knowledge would die with him. No K'da or Shontin would ever find this tomb.

The dust slowly began to clear from the air as Draycos worked, gradually settling into a soft coating that seemed to cling to every surface. The faint sounds of wildlife began to be heard, too, bird and insect twitterings as alien as the world they inhabited. Occasionally Draycos noticed his ears twitching as another new noise entered the mix, but he paid no conscious attention to the sounds. His entire focus was on the diamonds.

But all the concentration in the universe couldn't make up for what was no longer there. Damaged in the crash, the diamonds no longer held the full record of the ambush. Only bits and pieces remained, images here and there. Nothing he could use to positively identify the ships that had attacked them.

As slowly but inevitably as the settling of the dust around

him, he felt his strength begin to drain away. The data reader slipped first from his grasp, the diamonds themselves became too difficult to hold, and all too soon he found himself huddled on the deck beside Polphir's body. He was still three-dimensional, but as he gazed at the tips of his forepaws he thought he could see a hint of flattening in the ridges around the claw sheaths.

It was an odd sensation to be alone this way for so long. Much like the difference, he decided, between missing a meal and starving to death.

Still, on one level, it was only fair. All his friends and comrades were already dead. It was merely his turn to follow them.

And then, from somewhere aft of the command complex, he heard a sound.

At first it was so soft he thought it was his imagination. Even as it grew louder he was convinced his dying mind was simply playing tricks on him.

But no. It was real, all right. The sound of footsteps, coming toward him.

The attackers had arrived to finish the job.

Draycos took a deep breath. He would have time, maybe, for a single attack before either the weakness or their guns got him. A useless gesture, really.

But he was a warrior of the K'da. Better to die fighting than to do nothing at all.

Taking another breath, drawing together every bit of strength that still remained, he silently drew his legs beneath him and waited.

The footsteps came to the aft doorway. Draycos closed his eyes to slits; and then, suddenly, the intruder was there.

He was a human. No surprise there—the use of their contact's recognition signals had made it clear that their attackers either were humans or were allied with them. But aside from that single fact, he was not at all what Draycos was expecting.

He was young, for one thing, if his size was any indication. Humans and Shontine shared many physical similarities, and this human was no larger than a twelve-year-old Shontin boy.

Of course, Draycos had seen Shontine boys and girls that young pressed into military service in times of desperation. But it was clear that the boy standing in the doorway was no warrior. His clothing was all wrong, for one thing: no helmet, no body armor, no uniform. All he was wearing was a tan shirt and light blue pants, with low brown boots on his feet. He had a heavy-looking brown jacket slung over his shoulder; apparently it was warmer in here than he found comfortable.

He *was* at least armed, with what appeared to be a handgun belted at the left side of his waist. But the weapon was far too small to be a proper soldier's field gun. Besides that, a trained soldier should have had it ready in his hand when checking out enemy territory.

But if he wasn't one of the attackers, who was he?

"It's just like back there," the boy said, still standing in the doorway as he looked around the control complex. A trained warrior wouldn't stand that long in a doorway, either. "More of the same, only worse."

Draycos stayed motionless, struggling to understand the words. All the members of the advance team had learned the humans' chief trade language during the long voyage, but with his waning strength even something as simple as translation was becoming difficult. Perhaps he wouldn't have the strength for an attack after all.

"Wait a second," the boy said suddenly. "There *is* something new here."

"What is it?" a much fainter voice asked. Draycos looked around as best he could without moving his head, but he could see no one else. A communicator, then. An advance scout, perhaps, in contact with the true warrior coming behind him?

"Looks like a little dragon," the boy said, starting across the room toward Draycos. "No kidding—it really does. About the size of a small tiger, all covered with gold scales."

"Is it alive?"

"Doesn't look like it," the boy said, still moving forward. Almost within attack range now. "I suppose you want me to check."

"If you would be so kind," the other voice said. Draycos braced himself . . .

And for a moment the mental haze of his approaching death cleared, and a strange thought occurred to him.

Yes, he could attack this intruder as he'd planned. He could probably even kill the boy before he lost his hold on this universe and vanished into death and oblivion.

Or, instead, he could use that same last bit of strength to try to connect with him.

"Still not moving," the boy said. "I guess it's dead. Too bad—it's pretty neat looking. Huh—those gold scales have little bits of red on them, too, right at the edges. Cool."

It was a gamble, Draycos knew. A terrible, desperate gamble. Throughout their history, the K'da had met only two species who could act as hosts to them. There wasn't a chance in a hundred that these humans could do so.

And if the connection failed, there would be no attack. Draycos had strength enough for only a single action.

"Still not moving," the boy reported.

Draycos came to a decision. He was a K'da warrior, and he could not attack an untrained and unprepared opponent without clear cause. The boy stopped and leaned close. . . .

Draycos leaped.

CHAPTER 4

It was about the last thing Jack would ever have expected: for one of the "dead" bodies aboard the wrecked ship to suddenly come alive and charge at him. With a startled gasp he jumped backwards, reflexively throwing up an arm in front of his eyes. There was a flash of gold right in his face—he blinked—

And then, without a sound, it was gone. He spun around, nearly losing his balance on the litter-strewn deck.

The dragon had vanished.

Only then did he remember the tangler belted at his waist. He yanked out the weapon and popped off the safety catch, breathing hard and trembling with reaction as he looked wildly around. The dragon was gone, all right.

Only one small problem: there wasn't any place it could have gone to. It couldn't possibly have made it across the room and out the doorway back there, not in the half second it had taken Jack to turn around. With most everything solid in the room lying in broken piles on the floor, there was no place in the room itself for it to hide.

So where was it?

"Jack!" Uncle Virge's voice called urgently from the comm

clip on his shirt collar. "What is it? What's going on? Come on, lad, speak up."

"That dragon," Jack said. To his embarrassment, his voice was trembling. He hated when it did that. "It jumped at me. At least, I thought it did."

"What happened? Did it bite you? Claw you?"

"I—no, I don't think so," Jack said, still looking around. "I mean, I don't feel anything."

"Check your clothes," Uncle Virge ordered. "Look for rips or blood. Sometimes you don't feel injuries like that right away."

Jack glanced down at his shirt. "No, there's nothing. It just jumped at me and then disappeared."

"What do you mean, disappeared? Disappeared where?"

Jack didn't answer. The immediate shock of the incident was beginning to fade . . . and as it did so, he suddenly became aware that there was something odd about the way his skin felt. Almost as if there was a thin coating of paint or something on his chest and back.

He reached in under his shirt collar and touched his shoulder. It was skin, all right, normal everyday skin. It certainly didn't feel any different than usual to his fingertips. His back didn't feel any different, either, as he slid his hand down along his shoulder blade as far as it would go.

But the odd sensation persisted.

"Jack?"

"Hang on a second," Jack said, draping his leather jacket across the back of a broken chair and sliding his tangler back into its holster. Working a finger under the sealing seam running down the front of his shirt, he unsealed it and pulled it open.

He caught his breath. There, angling across his chest and stomach, was a wide golden band. It wrapped around his rib cage at both the top and bottom, disappearing around toward his back. Like a tuxedo cummerbund that hadn't been put on straight, he thought, or maybe the formal sash he'd sometimes seen military leaders wearing. There was texturing to it, too, he saw. A golden fish-scale pattern, with a sliver of red at the edge of each scale.

The same pattern as the vanished dragon.

A horrible thought struck him. Pulling the shirt free from his jeans, he slid it all the way off his right arm so that it was hanging on his left arm and shoulder. Twisting his head around, he looked down at his right shoulder.

To find himself gazing directly into the dragon's face.

"Ye-*oup!*" he yelped, jerking his head back and jumping three feet to his left.

It was like trying to jump away from his own body, and about as successful. The picture of the dragon didn't disappear or slide off or anything like that. It was still there, as if it had been painted on him.

Then, to his utter astonishment, the face rose slowly out of his skin, like the top of an alligator's head rising up through the surface of the water. The long upper jaw opened slightly, giving him a glimpse of sharp teeth—"Don't be afraid," a soft, snakelike voice said.

Jack screeched loud enough to hurt his own ears. His tangler was in his left hand, though he had no memory of having drawn it, and with all his strength he slammed the short barrel down on the dragon's head.

But the beast was too fast for him. It sank flat onto his skin again, and Jack's screech turned to a howl of pain as his attack succeeded only in bruising his own shoulder. Ignoring the pain, he struck again and again, stumbling sideways in a useless attempt to get away. Through the noise of his own panicked babbling, he was distantly aware that there were two different voices shouting at him.

He ignored them. Voices didn't matter. Nothing mattered but to somehow get this *thing* off him.

He was still flailing around when his foot caught on something and he toppled over onto his side.

Or rather, he should have toppled over onto his side. But even as he tried to get his arm around to break his fall, the feeling on his skin shifted, and something somehow broke his fall, setting him more or less gently onto the broken control board he'd been tumbling toward.

But gentle landing or not, the sudden fall snapped him out of his mindless attack on himself. Gasping for breath, he half sat, half lay there, his shoulder throbbing with the multiple blows he'd just brilliantly hammered down on it. In his left ear, he could hear Uncle Virge's voice shouting from the comm clip on his shirt collar, demanding to know what was happening.

In his right ear, the snakelike voice he'd heard earlier was speaking again.

"Everyone . . . shut . . . up," he ordered between gasps. "You hear me? Everyone just shut *up*."

Both voices went obediently silent. Jack took a few more breaths, trying desperately to calm down. His efforts were only a limited success. "All right," he said at last. "You—Voice Number Two—the one who isn't Uncle Virge. Who are you?"

"My name is Draycos," the snake voice replied from somewhere behind him, the sound tingling strangely against his skin.

Jack twisted around to look, but there was nothing there. The dragon head had disappeared from his shoulder, but out of the corner of his eye he could just see the tip of the snout further around on his back. "I am a poet-warrior of the K'da. Who are you?"

"I'm Jack Morgan," Jack said, his voice starting to shake again. Now for the *big* question. "*Where* are you?"

"Tell me first how you came to be aboard my ship," Draycos said. "Are you an enemy of the K'da and Shontine?"

"I'm not an enemy of anyone," Jack protested, scrambling back to his feet. "I saw your ship go down, and I came to check it out. That's all."

"Did you see our attackers?" The voice, Jack noted uneasily, moved with him, still tingling his shoulder.

"Well . . ." Jack hesitated, wondering how much to say. "We saw the battle," he said. "It looked like the guys in the little ships went aboard the big ones afterward. Are there more of your people up there?"

There was a soft sigh, even more snakelike than the voice. "They were my people," Draycos said. "They are all dead now."

"We don't know that," Jack said, feeling an obscure urge to be comforting. "Those Djinn-90s can't have had *that* many soldiers to put aboard."

"There is no one left to fight them," the dragon said sadly. "The K'da and Shontine were already dead."

"*All* of them?" Uncle Virge's voice asked, sounding surprised.

"All of them," Draycos said. "The weapon that was used against us kills all that it touches. It does not leave survivors."

Jack thought back to the purple tornadoes he'd seen playing

against the freighters' sides. A weapon that killed right through hull plates? "What about you?" he asked. "*You* survived."

"An unintended mercy," Draycos said. "We were already falling, and they thought merely to save themselves further effort."

Jack took a deep breath. It was pretty obvious by now what was going on. He still hoped he was wrong; but right or wrong, it was time to take the plunge and find out for sure. "You're on my back, aren't you?" he asked. "Wrapped around me like a—well, like a thin sheet of plastic."

"Yes," Draycos said.

"You're *what*?" Uncle Virge demanded. "You're *where*?"

"It's like he's a picture painted there," Jack said. "Or a full-body tattoo, like you see sometimes on Zhandig music stars."

"What do you mean, like a tattoo?" Uncle Virge said, sounding every bit as bewildered as Jack felt. "How can something alive be like a tattoo?"

"What, you think *I* know?" Jack shot back. "Look, if I could explain it—"

"Please," Draycos cut in. "Permit me."

Jack looked down. The dragon's head had slid back into view on his shoulder and was turning back and forth as if looking for something. "There," Draycos said. "That data reader."

"Where?" Jack asked, frowning at the debris.

A second later he jumped again as a sudden bit of extra weight came onto the back of his right arm, and a gold-scaled limb unexpectedly rose up out from that spot. A short finger or toe or whatever it was extended from the paw, pointing to a small flat instrument about three inches square lying among the debris on the deck. "There," Draycos said. "Go and kneel down beside it."

Swallowing, Jack obeyed. This was the very spot, he noted uneasily, where the dragon had been crouching when he came in. Could this thing be a weapon? "Now what?"

"I will give you a picture of what I am," Draycos said. "Do you see how the reader lies on the deck? Where they meet, the reader is a two-dimensional object. Do you agree?"

"Well, no, it's three-dimensional," Jack said. "It has length, width, and thickness."

"But it is two-dimensional where it meets the deck," Draycos repeated. "At that meeting, it has only length and width. Do you agree?"

Jack shrugged. "Fine. Whatever you say."

"It is not a matter of what I say," Draycos said, sounding impatient. "It is a matter of whether you understand. Consider the deck to be a two-dimensional universe, with the data reader as a two-dimensional object existing within it. There is no thickness there, only length and width. Two dimensions only. Do you understand?"

"I understood before," Jack said, a little impatience of his own starting to peek out through the heavy curtain of weirdness hanging over this whole thing. Having not been killed and eaten on the spot, he was starting to lose some of his initial fear, and he had better things to do than play word games with this Draycos character. "So what?"

"Very well," Draycos said. "Now lift the data reader so that one edge remains on the deck."

Jack did as instructed. "Okay. So?"

"In this picture, the data reader is still two-dimensional,"

Draycos said. "Yet to an observer within the two-dimensional universe of the deck, it now appears as a one-dimensional portion of a line. It has length only, but no width. The part that would give it width has lifted away along a third dimension."

Jack stared down at the reader, a funny tingling sensation creeping across the skin at the back of his neck. Was Draycos saying what he thought he was saying? "Are you trying to tell me," he asked slowly, "that you're really three-dimensional, but that you somehow became *two*-dimensional? Just plain flat? And then that you somehow pasted yourself across my back?"

"I am still three-dimensional," Draycos said. "As with the data reader, most of my body is now projected along a fourth dimension, outside the bounds of this universe."

On Jack's left shoulder, the comm clip had gone silent. Apparently, even Uncle Virge couldn't think of anything to say to this one. That was a bad sign. "No," Jack said. "Sorry, but this doesn't make any sense at all."

"Yet I am here," Draycos reminded him.

"No," Jack said firmly. He turned his eyes away to the left, away from the dragon head staring up at him from his right shoulder. "This isn't real. It can't be real. It's some kind of trick."

"Why would I wish to trick you?" Draycos asked, sliding around Jack's back to his left shoulder and again looking up at him. "What purpose would it serve?"

"Stop *doing* that!" Jack snapped, twisting his head back the other way. Reaching around, he pulled the hanging sleeve back around and got his right arm into it. "I don't know why. What purpose does anything serve? What do you want?"

"I want that which all beings desire," Draycos told him. "Life."

"And what, you can't live anywhere except my back?" Jack demanded sarcastically.

"No," Draycos said. "I cannot."

Jack had been about to fasten his shirt's sealing strip again. Now he paused, frowning down at the gold scales on his chest. "What do you mean?"

"The K'da are not like other beings, Jack Morgan," the dragon said. "We cannot run freely for longer than six of your hours at a time. After that we must return to this two-dimensional form and rest against a host body."

"Or?" Jack prompted.

"If we do not have a host, we fade away and die," Draycos said. "I was nearly dead when you appeared. Your arrival, plus the fortunate fact that your species is able to serve as a K'da host, has saved my life. For this I thank you."

"You're welcome," Jack said automatically. "Not like I had a choice. So, what, you're some kind of parasite?"

"I do not know that word."

"A parasite is something that feeds off its host organism," Jack explained. "It takes food or something else it needs from the host."

"I take nothing from my host," Draycos said. "I must use the surface of my host's body, but that is all."

"You take away his privacy," Jack pointed out.

"I offer companionship and protection in return," Draycos said. "For that reason, we consider ourselves to be symbionts with our hosts, not . . . parasites. But perhaps you do not consider that a fair exchange. Does your species require more loneliness than I understood?"

"We all like to be alone every so often," Jack said gruffly, trying to hide the sudden pang of emotion. *Loneliness*. Whether he'd meant to or not, the dragon had touched a painful nerve with that one. "So why me? Why didn't you wrap yourself around a tree or something?"

"It does not work that way," Draycos said. "We must have a proper host. I do not know what it is that makes one species acceptable and another not. Perhaps none of the K'da do."

"Oh," Jack said, for lack of anything better to say. "So . . . what now?"

"That is your decision," Draycos said. "Do you wish me to leave?"

The obvious answer—*yes!*—unexpectedly got stuck in Jack's throat. "If I said yes, where would you go?" he asked instead. "I mean, there's no one here but me."

"After six hours had passed, I would die," Draycos said softly. "But I am a warrior of the K'da. I will not force myself upon you if you do not wish it."

"Yeah," Jack muttered, hunching his shoulders with indecision. Intriguing though this might be, he still had troubles of his own. The last thing he could afford right now was to take on passengers.

Especially a passenger who looked like a bright gold dragon. That was definitely *not* the way to keep a low profile. "Look, Draycos—"

"Before you decide, I must add one other piece of information," the dragon said. "The reason we are standing amid the wreckage of my ship is that my people were attacked. Moreover, we were attacked by the ultimate weapon of the Valahgua, our mortal enemies."

Jack shook his head. "Never heard of them. Uncle Virge?"

"No reference on the books," the other said.

"I would not expect you to know of them," Draycos said.

"Like us, they live a long way from here. Our voyage took nearly two years, human measure, and carried us across a great void of space."

"You mean like from another spiral arm?" Jack hazarded, trying to visualize the map of the Milky Way galaxy from the limited and highly informal schooling Uncle Virgil had given him between jobs. All of explored space, both the human-colonized regions as well as all the other known alien species and planets, lay along the broad band of stars called the Orion Arm. To get here from outside that band would be quite a trip.

"That is correct," Draycos confirmed. "We came in hopes of fleeing the Valahgua and their terrible weapon. Yet the weapon was here waiting for us."

"They must have followed you."

"Impossible," Draycos said. "As I said, their weapon was here ahead of us."

"And on human-designed ships, too," Uncle Virge pointed out. "Unless your Valahgua fly Djinn-90s."

"The only explanation was that we were betrayed," Draycos said. "You have to help me find those responsible."

"Oh, no I don't," Jack retorted. "Look, I'm sorry your people got nailed. But this isn't any of my business."

"You are wrong," Draycos said firmly. "The Death chooses no favorites, be they Shontine or K'da or human. There is no defense against it, and there is no bargaining with the Valahgua. If they have formed a secret alliance with one of the species in this region, all of your people are in deadly danger."

"What do you mean, no defense?" Uncle Virge asked.

"There is no material that can block the weapon," Draycos said. "Its range is short, but all within that range die. We must bring warning to your people."

Jack made a face. "Yes, well, that might be a little difficult," he said. "You see—"

"Quiet!" Draycos cut him off suddenly.

"What?" Jack whispered.

"Footsteps," Draycos whispered back. "Someone is coming."

CHAPTER 5

Jack was still holding the alien data reader. Flipping up his shirttail, he stuffed the gadget into one of the back pockets of his jeans. "How many?" he whispered.

"Only one set of footsteps," Draycos murmured back. The dragon head had again lifted out of Jack's shoulder, the long snout poking out under the edge of the shirt. "He moves cautiously, like a warrior."

"Or a cop," Jack muttered, crossing as silently as he could to the chair where he'd hung his jacket. He couldn't hear the footsteps himself, but he didn't doubt the dragon's pointy little ears for a minute. "Any other way out of here?"

"There is the bubble," Draycos said. The snout lifted to point toward the ceiling. "But the ladder is no longer secure."

Jack looked up as he got his arms into his jacket sleeves. It was a good twenty feet up to the first landing, plus another ten feet to a second landing and then the broken glass of the bubble. And the ladder did indeed look pretty rickety.

But the chance of a two-story fall was still better than tangling with a trained soldier. Or with a cop. "I'll risk it," he said, shifting direction toward the ladder. He reached it, got a grip on the uprights—

"Solidify!" a hard, flat voice snapped from the doorway behind him.

Jack froze in place, wincing. Caught like a rat in a box; and he still hadn't heard any footsteps. Whoever this guy was, he was way too good for Jack's liking. "Don't shoot," he called, putting some near-panic into his voice. "Please don't shoot."

"Turn around," the voice ordered. "Keep your hands up."

Jack obeyed, turning just far enough to keep his right shoulder toward the newcomer. The tangler belted at his left hip was a short-range weapon, and he wanted to keep it his little secret as long as possible.

The figure standing just inside the room to the right of the doorway was big and wide and definitely not human. He was a Brummga, most of his round face obscured by his helmet. He was dressed in a mismatched collection of ground-soldier combat gear, with a dark red helmet, blue protector vest, and green combat fatigues. A small orange medkit hung from the left side of his belt beside some kind of wand in a narrow, brown-and-white-striped holster. The combined effect of his body shape and the colorful outfit made him look rather comical.

But there was nothing funny about the shoulder-slung weapon pointed in Jack's direction. It was black and shiny and nasty looking, and would probably make a serious mess if the Brummga pulled the trigger. Whatever thoughts Jack might have had about using his tangler vanished quietly into the morning mists.

But he had to do *something*. If these Valahgua guys Draycos had mentioned didn't want any witnesses to their attack, a

Brummga was just the sort of boneheaded hatchetman to cheerfully clean the plate for them. Jack's only hope was to convince the Brummga that he knew absolutely nothing about what was going on.

"Who are you?" the Brummga demanded. "What are you doing here?"

"I didn't mean anything," Jack pleaded, using the frightened-child whine that Uncle Virgil had found so useful on so many jobs. "I saw the ship and just wanted to see if there was anything I could use. I didn't mean anything."

"How did you see the ship?" the Brummga asked. "Where did you come from?"

"Right over there," Jack said, waving vaguely off to the side. "We've got a little place off in the forest."

The alien made a sound like a bass drum being attacked by a gang of chipmunks. "How many of you are there?" he demanded, starting across the room toward Jack. "What did you see?"

"What do you mean?" Jack asked, trying to sound bewildered. It wasn't easy to out-stupid a Brummga, but he was determined to give it his best shot. "We saw this ship. I told you that."

"*Before* you saw the ship," the Brummga growled. He was close enough now for Jack to see that his fatigues carried no military rank badges or insignia. "What happened *before*?"

"Well, there was a lot of *noise*," Jack huffed, as if that should be obvious, still keeping his right shoulder toward the Brummga as the other approached. The tangler was no longer an option, not with that gun pointed at his chest. But his shirt and jacket were still open in front, and the last thing he wanted was to let the other get a clear view of Draycos wrapped around his chest. "What do you mean, what happened?"

"Did you see anything up in space?" the Brummga asked. "Were you watching up into space?"

Jack blinked. "Into *space*?" he asked. Along the left side of his rib cage, the side away from the Brummga, he could again feel the flowing-paint sensation as Draycos stealthily changed position.

If the dragon was getting restless with the conversation, he wasn't the only one. "You ask many questions," the Brummga rumbled, his ugly face turning even uglier. "But you don't answer any. Maybe you need help with your mouth."

"Look, I didn't mean anything," Jack said, putting a little more whine into his voice as he tried desperately to come up with a good story. The Brummga was only four steps away. Another few seconds, and Jack was probably going to find that big ugly gun pressed up against his cheek. If he didn't come up with something before then—

Without warning, a horrible scream pierced the air.

It was a sound like Jack had never heard before, and in that single terrifying second he hoped he would never hear it again. It was like the cry of a screech owl twisted together with the howl of a hunting wolf, with the wail of a banshee from Uncle Virgil's old Irish legends thrown into the mix. It seemed to come from everywhere and from nowhere, bouncing around the room and threatening to bring down the rest of the glass from the broken bubble above them.

The Brummga reacted instantly, dropping into a crouch and swinging his gun around to point at the doorway behind him.

And as he turned away from Jack, there was a sudden surge of movement and weight at Jack's back, and a twitching at his holster. The weight disappeared as something fell from beneath his shirt. Jack twisted his head around, just in time to see Draycos land silently on the deck behind him . . .

With Jack's tangler clutched in his front paws.

There was a soft *chuff*; and an instant later the tangler cartridge burst against the Brummga's upper back, sending hundreds of thick, milky-white threads bursting outward. The threads whipped around him, wrapping themselves around his torso, head, and arms like an instant spiderweb.

He howled, staggering off balance as he tried to turn around. But he was way too late. Even as he spun back, his gun pointing mostly upward where the tangle of threads had trapped it, the cocoon completed itself. With a brief flash, the capacitor built into the cartridge discharged, sending a jolt of stunning electric current through its captive. The Brummga gave a pitiful doglike yelp, toppled over onto the deck, and lay still.

Draycos was already in motion, bounding over to the fallen mercenary and giving him a quick examination. "An interesting weapon," he commented, turning back to Jack. "We had best get moving."

It took Jack two tries to find his voice. "Right," he managed. "That was . . . was that you?"

"A K'da battle cry," Draycos said, flipping the tangler to Jack. "It seemed a reasonable diversion. Are you ready?"

"I'm three blocks past ready," Jack said, dropping the weapon back into its holster.

"Pardon?"

"Skip it," Jack said. "The ladder?"

"Yes," Draycos confirmed, turning his glittering green eyes upward toward the bubble. "When I say." Crouching down, he leaped.

Jack followed him with his eyes, feeling his mouth drop open. Twenty feet straight up, and the dragon made it with a foot or two to spare. Twisting around, catlike, on the narrow landing, he got his front paws firmly wrapped around the upper part of the ladder. "Now; come," he said.

"Hang on," Jack said, kneeling down beside the unconscious Brummga as a sudden thought struck him.

"What are you doing?" Draycos demanded.

"Trying to get this thing out," Jack told him, digging into the tangler webbing over the long holstered wand lying along the mercenary's left leg.

"An unknown weapon is dangerous to use," Draycos warned.

"You mean like my tangler?" Jack retorted. "You seemed to handle that just fine."

"I am a K'da warrior," Draycos said stiffly. "The understanding and use of weapons is my profession."

"You're still lucky I hadn't put the safety catch back on," Jack grunted. "Don't worry, a slapstick's the easiest thing in the world to use. You press the button at your end and touch the other guy with the other end, and he won't be bothering you for a couple of hours. Rats."

"What?"

"It's buried too deep under the webbing," Jack said, standing up again. "Never mind. Here I come."

Even with the dragon bracing the top, the ladder felt pretty shaky. He didn't want to think what it would have been like without the extra support.

But the ladder held, and so did the one to the upper control area. The lower section of the dome wasn't as badly crunched as it had looked from below, but there were several gaps big enough for them to get through. A minute later, they were standing outside on the top of the ship.

"Where is your spacecraft?" Draycos asked.

"Way back there," Jack said, pointing toward the forested areas to the right. "There's a crack in the hull about fifty yards back where I came in."

"Good," Draycos said. "Quickly, then."

They headed off. The damage wasn't as bad up here as it had been along the sides of the hull, Jack noted, but the handful of trees lining both sides more than made up for it. Most of them had been smashed into toothpicks as the ship plowed through the area, and those that remained standing had been knocked about at crazy angles. Mostly they were leaning away from the ship, but a few were actually leaning toward it.

Everything within sight, trees and ground alike, had been scorched and blackened by the heat of the crash. They were probably lucky the crash hadn't sparked a forest fire.

From the direction of the wrecked bubble behind them came the faint sound of crunching metal. Jack spun around, tangler in hand, but no one was visible. "You think the ladder went down?" he hazarded.

"With some assistance, yes," Draycos agreed. "I believe the pursuit has begun. Come; over here."

He veered suddenly toward the edge, aiming toward a tree that was leaning inward. "Wait a second," Jack said, frowning, as he turned to follow. "The *Essenay*'s still further back."

"If we remain here, they will have a very limited search area," Draycos explained over his shoulder. "On the ground our chances of eluding them are greater."

"Yeah, but it's forty feet to the ground," Jack objected. "There was a ladder built into the hull near where I came in— let's use that."

"All ladders will be watched," Draycos said. "This they may not expect."

"Right," Jack muttered, throwing a dubious look at the tree they were making for. Leaning toward the ship, yes, but at its closest it was still a good ten feet away. "I suppose it's too late to mention that my species doesn't jump nearly as well as yours does."

"Do not worry," Draycos said, trotting to a halt beside the tree at the point where the hull started its downward curve. This time he didn't even bother to crouch, but just jumped from a standing start over to the tree.

For a second he hung there, all four feet clinging to the tree with claws Jack hadn't noticed before. Then, turning his head, he peered back toward Jack. "Leap when I say," he said. "Ready—"

With a convulsive jerk, the dragon pushed away with his hind legs and arched his whole body backwards, like a reversed vid of how he'd landed on the tree in the first place. The arching continued until he was stretched straight back toward Jack. His tail uncurled and stiffened—"Leap," Draycos ordered.

If Jack had stopped to think, he never would have done it. To jump to the tail of an unknown alien as it hung from a fire-damaged tree was an amazingly stupid thing to do.

But all he could think about at the moment was the tangled Brummga and his buddies. He jumped as ordered, caught the gold-scaled tail, and a second later slammed against the black-ened tree trunk as the dragon collapsed back to vertical again.

"Can you climb down from here?" Draycos asked.

"Sure," Jack said, breathing hard as he shifted his grip from the dragon's slippery tail to the tree itself. He hadn't managed to get his feet up in front of him in time, and the impact had knocked a fair amount of the wind out of him. Fortunately, his jacket had protected him from the worst of the scrapes he might otherwise have collected. Taking a couple of deep breaths to steady himself, he started down.

Most of the branches had been splintered or knocked off by the ship's crash, but there were enough limb stumps still sticking out to provide hand and footholds. Draycos, having swiveled around on the tree until he was facedown like a squirrel, passed him going down the opposite side of the trunk.

Two minutes later, they were on the ground. "Where now?" Draycos asked.

Jack looked around, orienting himself as he brushed the worst of the soot off his hands. "This way," he told the dragon, angling off through the scorch zone. "There's a small clearing we were able to put down in, just past that ridge over there. Uncle Virge?"

"The ship's ready," Uncle Virge's voice came from his comm clip. "Better hurry. If the amount of ground-radio traffic is anything to go by, they're starting to heat up the search for you."

Jack nodded grimly. Terrific. "Right," he said. "Here we come."

CHAPTER 6

The ridge Jack was headed for was yet another result of the crash: a mound of smoking dirt that had been thrown up by the big ship as it plowed across the ground. Most of the smaller trees in this zone had been knocked over as the dirt swept past, but there were enough of the larger ones sticking out at all angles to make navigation hazardous. Earlier, on his way toward the wreck, Jack had nearly run into at least three of them in the dense smoke, and he'd been able to feel the burning heat of the dirt itself right through his boots.

Now, as they angled toward the ridge going the other direction, it didn't look a whole lot more inviting. What Draycos and his bare paws were going to think of it he didn't know.

It didn't take long for him to find out. Only a few steps into the smoke Draycos, who had been in the lead, paused and let Jack catch up. A silent leap, a brief weight on Jack's chest which quickly vanished, and Jack was slogging his way through the crumbly dirt alone.

He continued on, fighting hard not to cough as he waded through the smoke, feeling more than a little annoyed. The least the dragon could have done, he grumbled to himself, would have been to ask permission before climbing aboard.

He had gone perhaps ten paces more, and was passing a particularly large tree trunk that had managed to stay mostly vertical, when a pair of arms reached out from behind the tree and wrapped themselves solidly around his chest. "Gotcha!" a deep human voice said.

"Ye-*oup*!" Jack gasped, trying to pull away. A *human* voice? "Hey!"

The man responded by lifting him completely clear of the ground. "Oh, no you don't," he growled. "Settle down or I'll break your ribs."

"No, no, let me go," Jack pleaded, still fighting against the grip as he flailed his legs around helplessly. It was no use; the man was as strong as an ox. "Help! Mommy!"

"Oh, shut up," the man snarled contemptuously. He shifted grip slightly, and there was a soft click from somewhere behind Jack's ear. "Base, this is Dumbarton. I've got him."

"Do you need assistance?" a fainter voice demanded.

Jack stiffened, a chill running through him despite the sweltering heat of the ridge. Earlier, he had thought of Draycos's voice as being snakelike, which made sense now that he knew the dragon's reptilian nature.

But for absolute snakelike quality, this new voice beat Draycos hands down. It was human, but as cold and heartless and just plain nasty a voice as Jack had ever heard.

Considering some of the people he and Uncle Virgil had kept company with over the years, that was saying a lot.

"Negative, sir," Dumbarton said. His tone was suddenly respectful, and Jack had the odd sense that this wasn't who he'd expected to answer the comm clip. "Like the Brummy said, he's just a kid, maybe twelve or thirteen. I can handle him."

"He was alone?"

"Yes, sir," Dumbarton said.

"Very well," the evil voice said. "Bring him here. The rest of you, spread out and continue the search. I want his ship, or his house, or wherever it is he came from. *And* I want everyone who's still there."

There was a series of faint acknowledgments. "Okay, kid, let's go," Dumbarton said, swinging Jack around toward the wrecked ship. As he did so, Jack felt a brief tug of extra weight down by his left hip. "You want to walk on your own, or—?"

He never finished the question. From behind Jack came the faint crackle of an electrical discharge; and without warning, Dumbarton's grip loosened, and Jack found himself dropping through the encircling arms to land flat on his rear in the blazing hot dirt.

Stifling a yelp, he scrambled to his feet, legs and rear end feeling flash-toasted even through his jeans. Dumbarton was sprawled on his back, his eyes shut, his mouth hanging half open. Beside him on the ground, humming softly as it automatically recharged itself, lay his slapstick.

"About time," Jack muttered, wincing as he brushed the bits of dirt off his rear.

There was a sudden burst of gold in front of his face, and Draycos leaped into view, landing on the ground beside the fallen man. A quick slash of his claws, and the comm clip on the man's shoulder went spinning away into the smoke. "I apologize for the delay," the dragon said. "I had hoped that with your capture they would call off the search. That would have given us more time."

"No, they want the complete package," Jack said. Still, for

a lizard, this Draycos was pretty smart. "Let's not wait till they figure out that they don't even have me," he added, pulling open his jacket and shirt and offering Draycos his chest. "Get aboard and let's go."

To his surprise, Draycos stepped instead behind Dumbarton and began digging with his front paws into the hot dirt beneath the man's shoulders. "First help me move him to this tree," the dragon said.

Jack blinked. "Why?"

"Because he might otherwise burn to death," Draycos explained. He had a grip on the man's shoulders now and was straining to lift him up. "At the very least, his hands and neck will be severely burned."

"I thought he killed your people," Jack protested. "What do you care if he dies or not?"

"I am a warrior of the K'da," Draycos said firmly as he started to drag the man back toward the nearest tree trunk. "We kill only when necessary, and in battle. We do not slaughter helpless enemies."

"He was sure going to help them kill *us*, you know," Jack reminded him.

"Will you help me, or not?"

Jack shook his head in disgust. "I don't believe this," he said under his breath. But he stepped to Draycos's side and took one of the man's arms. A minute later they had him propped up against the tree, his head sagging onto his chest, his hands lying in his lap out of the dirt. "There," Jack said, stepping back. "Happy?"

"It will do," Draycos said. Brushing the dirt off his front paws, he leaped up at Jack and flattened himself out around his torso again. "Now: to your ship."

"Assuming there's still a ship to go to," Jack muttered, slapping his hands against sudden hot spots on his chest and stomach. His first thought was that the heat was coming from Draycos himself, but he saw now that it was merely bits of dirt that had been clinging to Draycos's back paws, dirt that had been left behind when the dragon went two-dimensional.

This whole thing, he decided, was definitely going to take some getting used to.

"Will your companion not defend it?" Draycos asked from his now customary headrest on Jack's right shoulder.

"Not very well," Jack told him. "Just keep your fingernails crossed."

"Pardon?"

"Skip it," Jack said, scooping up Dumbarton's slapstick and stuffing it through the back of his belt where it would be handy if he needed it. Or, more likely, if Draycos needed it. "Come on."

They reached the top of the ridge without seeing or hearing anyone else and started down. Here, outside the crash zone, the forest was alive with color, bright reds and yellows splashed against more subdued blues and blue-greens. Spindly bushes shared space with the thick-trunked trees, along with the curly-fry grass that seemed to grow everywhere on this part of Iota Klestis. Here and there Jack caught a glimpse of a bird or large insect flying about on its own business.

"Is that your ship?" Draycos murmured as Jack crouched down behind one of the bushes and gave the area a quick study. "The group of bushes at the far edge of the clearing against a line of trees?"

"That's it," Jack said sourly. "Only it's not supposed to be that easy to see."

It certainly wasn't to him, anyway. To his eyes, the *Essenay*'s outline was only barely visible along the edges of what seemed to be a group of bushes and grasses swaying gently in the breeze. The only reason he could see it at all was because he knew exactly where to look.

So naturally Draycos, freshly arrived in the Orion Arm and who knew nothing about anything, had picked it out of the background without a second glance. So much for the big, fancy chameleon hull-wrap Uncle Virgil had installed two years ago.

"It is quite well concealed," Draycos assured him. "My eyes accept slightly different wavelengths of light than yours do, and your camouflage does not exactly duplicate them. Also, as a warrior, I am trained to search for hidden objects."

"A handy talent," Jack growled. "Let's just hope our buddies back there don't include anyone like you."

Still no one in sight. Either they were all off searching a different part of the forest, or they'd already found the *Essenay* and were lying in ambush for whoever might show up there.

Either way, there was nothing to be gained by sitting here waiting. "Okay, we're going whole hog," he muttered to Draycos. "Hang on."

Taking a deep breath, he gathered his feet under him and sprinted toward the ship.

If there was an ambush waiting, it was a rotten one. No one shot at him as he slipped between the trees and pounded into the open area of the clearing. He kept going, hoping he wouldn't catch a foot on something hidden in the grass and end up face-first on the ground.

He was about thirty feet from the *Essenay* when the airlock hatch slid open and the gangway extended itself outward. Jack braced himself, wondering if that was the signal the hidden attackers had been waiting for.

But there was still no reaction from the surrounding forest. A second later he was charging up the gangway, ducking his head under the hatchway, trying to skid to a halt before he slammed full-tilt into the bulkhead on the far side of the narrow airlock.

Draycos had already anticipated the problem. Again, the sudden telltale weight appeared on his chest as Draycos came up and off him, putting all four legs straight out in front of Jack like gold-scaled shock absorbers to help absorb the impact.

Between the four K'da legs and two human arms, they bounced safely together off the bulkhead. "Close the hatch," Jack snapped as he regained his balance. Draycos dropped all the way off him, his long neck swiveling around as he checked things out. "Uncle Virge?" Jack called again.

"All right, all right, I'm not deaf," Uncle Virge said, his voice sounding odd as the hatch slid closed. "I take it this is your new friend?"

"Draycos, meet Uncle Virge," Jack said, slapping the door pad. The inner hatch slid open, and he headed forward at a dead run. A glance over his shoulder showed Draycos was right behind him.

He reached the cockpit, tossed his leather jacket and the slapstick in a corner, and slid into the pilot seat. The preflight had been done, he saw, and Uncle Virge had computed an ECHO course for use once they were outside the atmosphere.

The weapons panel, he noted with decidedly mixed feelings, had also been activated. Uncle Virgil had taught him how to use it, but he'd never even had to turn it on, let alone actually shoot at anyone.

"How may I best serve?" Draycos asked. He was standing behind Jack on his back paws, his body stretched upward with his front paws braced on the back of the chair. His pointed snout was swinging back and forth over Jack's shoulder as he studied the controls.

"You can't," Jack said, getting a grip on the Y-shaped control yoke. "This is a one-man operation. Hang onto something; here we go."

Without waiting for a reply, he threw power to the antigrav lifters. The *Essenay* shuddered once, then lurched up and out of the clearing. They cleared the trees, Jack switched over from the lifters to the main drive, and they were off.

As the ship headed up through the drifting smoke, he felt a brief weight on his shoulders, then nothing. The dragon had found something to hang onto, all right. Him.

"They will send ships to intercept," Draycos warned from Jack's right shoulder. "Is this vessel armed?"

"Right here," Jack said, letting go of the yoke with his left hand long enough to tap the weapons panel. Getting a two-handed grip on the yoke again, he turned the *Essenay* into a tight right-hand curve. "We've got two meteor-defense lasers and a short-range particle-beam shredder. And four small missile launchers."

"Jack!" Uncle Virge protested. "The missiles are privileged information, lad."

"What, you think he's not going to notice when we fire them?" Jack retorted.

"Instruct me in its operation," the dragon said, the top of his head rising up out of Jack's skin for a better look.

Jack shook his head. "No, that's all right," he said, risking a quick look at the aft sensor display. Was that a small ship rising from the forest near the wrecked freighter?

"Instruct me in its operation," Draycos insisted. "I am a warrior of the K'da—"

"Yeah, yeah, I remember," Jack cut him off. No, it wasn't a small ship coming up from the forest. It was *two* small ships. Terrific. "No offense, but so far all I've seen you do is grab other people's weapons. Any good pickpocket could do that."

"Have you ever engaged in combat?" Draycos countered. "Have you ever flown this spacecraft in combat?"

"No, and no," Jack ground out. Already the two ships were gaining on him. Fighter-sized, he could see now. Probably fighter-armed, too. "Now shut up and let me fly. This is hard enough as it is."

In answer, his open shirt was suddenly shoved back off his left shoulder, and a pair of golden legs sprouted from his skin there. "Hey!" he snapped as the unexpected weight translated into a brief wobble of the control yoke. "Watch it!"

"You cannot fly and defend together," Draycos said firmly, the extended paws poised over the weapons panel. "You are not trained, and these controls are not well laid out. Now instruct me."

Jack muttered a word that had once cost him a week of desserts. To trust his life to someone else, and an alien newcomer at that . . .

But the dragon was right. Besides, he could hardly be any worse at this than Jack was. "All right, fine," he said, trying to coax a little more speed out of the engines. "The left section handles targeting. The way you work it . . ."

The quick course took a minute and a half, about the same time it took the two fighters to close to firing range. Jack could only hope the dragon was a quick study.

"Interesting," Draycos commented as the fighters approached. "They are using a classic *chiv-nez* maneuver."

"I guess word gets around," Jack said, squeezing the control yoke hard as he studied the aft display. The fighters weren't going to wait long before making their move, he knew. Probably deciding how best to disable the *Essenay* without blowing it completely out of the sky.

Unless, of course, Snake Voice had changed his mind about wanting his prisoners undamaged. In that case, the fighters' job was going to be a whole lot easier.

"You mistake my point," Draycos said. "I do not know whether they borrowed the maneuver from the K'da or created it themselves. What I do know is how to deal with it. At my command, make the tightest turn to the left this ship is capable of."

Jack frowned. Turning left would put them directly into the path of one of the fighters. "Uncle Virge?"

"Sorry, lad, but I can't see anything better to suggest," Uncle Virge said. "We'll never make it out of the atmosphere before they catch us. Let's see what tricks our K'da warrior can pull out of his hat."

Jack took a deep breath. "Okay," he said. "Okay, I'm ready."

"Very well," Draycos said, his breath uncomfortably hot on Jack's cheek. On the aft display the fighters had finished their study of the situation and were starting to move in. "Prepare . . . now."

Jack twisted the yoke all the way to the left, leaning into the turn as the *Essenay* skidded hard to the side. At the same time, he heard the short spitting hiss of one of their missiles being launched.

"Draycos!" Uncle Virge shouted. "Idiot—you fired too low!"

Draycos didn't reply. The *Essenay* started to buck inside its own shock wave; Jack leaned hard on the yoke to control it, his full attention on the wind-skid indicators. If they went into a stall now, the ship would be a sitting duck.

From the weapons board came another spitting hiss, followed immediately by the flicker of the cockpit lights that meant the lasers were firing. "Draycos, either learn to shoot straight or stop wasting our missiles," Uncle Virge snapped. "All you're doing is—"

He broke off suddenly. Jack had just enough time to frown; and then, from the corner of his eye he saw a brilliant flash. "What happened?" he snapped, shifting his attention back to the aft display. The explosion was already starting to fade, and in its light he could see scattered bits of debris flying outward in all directions.

"I will be dipped in butter and rolled in bread crumbs," Uncle Virge said, sounding awed. "It worked. It actually worked."

"What worked?" Jack demanded. "I wasn't watching. What happened?"

"Your gold-plated friend and his near-misses suckered one of the fighters into flying straight into his friend, that's all," Uncle Virge said. "Amazing."

"They were too close together," Draycos added, his forelegs pulling back and settling flat onto Jack's skin. "The *chivnez* maneuver has always had that weakness."

On the ECHO section of the board, a green light flashed. "We're clear of atmosphere," Jack announced. "Should I put us on ECHO?"

"By all means," Uncle Virge said. "Before they get something else into the air after us."

Jack nodded and pulled the short lever. The shimmering rainbow effect flashed in front of them and became the blue of hyperspace.

For the moment, at least, they were safe.

CHAPTER 7

Dinner that evening was a simple affair.

It was simple for Jack, anyway. It was somewhat hit-or-miss for Draycos. The dragon had never sampled human fare before, and even with the *Essenay*'s food synthesizer churning out small test samples at its usual speed and efficiency, the process took quite awhile.

Fortunately, basic nutrition wasn't going to be a problem. According to Draycos, the K'da body could synthesize all the vitamins he needed from the basic proteins and carbohydrates of a standard human diet. The trick was more a matter of finding something he wouldn't turn up his pointy snout at.

They finally hit on a combination of hamburger and tuna fish, mixed together with chocolate sauce and a dash of light-grade motor oil from the *Essenay*'s engine room. Draycos ate dog-style, scooping the meal up with teeth and tongue from a soup bowl at one end of the short galley table.

Jack sat at the other end, eating his cheeseburger and trying hard not to think about the weird combination the dragon was chomping down.

When dinner was over, it was time to retire to the dayroom

with a glass of fizzy-soda for Jack and a bowl of orange-flavored water for Draycos. For a long, hard discussion.

"I'm sorry," Jack said after the dragon had related his version of the battle. "I know you want to get back at the people who killed your friends. But I really can't help you."

"You misunderstand me, Jack Morgan," Draycos said. He was lying on the dayroom floor on his stomach, his posture halfway between that of a dog and a cat. "I do not seek revenge. I do not even seek justice."

"Then what *do* you want?" Jack asked.

"I have told you already," Draycos said. "I must find those who used the Death against us."

"But if you don't want revenge—"

"Tell us more about this Death weapon," Uncle Virge's voice came from the intercom speaker. "You say it kills other beings besides K'da and Shontine. How do you know?"

"We have seen it used against others," Draycos said, the tip of his tail lashing restlessly through the air behind him. "The Valahgua are a vicious people who seek total domination of our region of space. They have already destroyed one species and scattered two others who stood in the way of that goal. The K'da and Shontine are only their most recent victims. Why do you not believe me?"

The intercom gave a soft sigh. "We find it hard to believe for the simple fact that it sounds unbelievable," Uncle Virge said candidly. "I mean, come *on*. A weapon that goes straight through a ship's hull without damaging it, yet kills everyone inside? How can that be possible?"

"I do not know the science," Draycos said. "It is said that the Death is a vibration of space itself, which seeks out the center core of all living beings and destroys that connection and their harmony with the universe."

"That must be the poet part of the poet-warrior coming out," Jack murmured, sipping his fizzy-soda.

"I do not know the proper words," Draycos said impatiently. "I know only the reality. If the Death has come to this region of space, your people are in great danger. Why can you not understand that?"

"We understand just fine," Uncle Virge said quietly. "Trouble is, there's something you're holding back. Something important that you're not telling us."

For a moment Draycos lay as unmoving as a statue. Then, the tip of his tail twitched again. "Very well," he said. "Let us trade secrets."

His tongue flicked out between his teeth. "You may start, Jack Morgan. Tell me why you pretend there is another human aboard this ship."

Jack felt his throat tighten. "What are you talking about?" he asked, the automatic caution of long habit kicking in. "I already explained that Uncle Virge is an invalid and can't leave his cabin."

"Do not lie to me," Draycos warned. "All beings, whether K'da or Shontine or human, leave traces of their scent in the air. There is no second human here."

"Oh, really?" Uncle Virge said huffily. "Let me tell you, my gold-scaled friend. You have a lot to learn about us humans—"

"No," Jack cut him off. After a year of deception, he was suddenly tired of the lies. Tired of *all* the lies. "No, it's all right. He's got us. I mean, he's got me."

"Jack, lad—"

"No," Jack said firmly. "He saved my life. He deserves to know."

He turned to Draycos. "Uncle Virge is a computer program," he told the dragon. "It's the standard ship's computer interface; only before he died, my Uncle Virgil imprinted it with his own voice and speech mannerisms."

"Interesting," Draycos murmured. "Is it alive?"

"Not like us, no," Jack said. "He can mimic a person when he talks, and he can think and reason a little. But not very much, and not outside his programming."

"I see." Draycos was silent a moment. "How long have you lived this way?"

"About a year," Jack said. "Uncle Virgil died in a . . . well, it was sort of an accident."

"And you have been alone ever since?"

Jack shrugged. "It's not so bad. I don't get lonely much. Anyway, it wasn't like he had a lot of time for me even before that."

Draycos's ears twitched. "And why is it important that this be kept a secret?"

"Because I'm only fourteen years old," Jack said, hearing the old bitterness creeping into his voice. "According to the all-wise, all-knowing Internos fusspots, that's too young for someone to be flying alone out here. If they found out, they'd take the *Essenay* away from me and put me in some group home somewhere."

"Would that not be better for you?"

"I don't want it," Jack snapped. "And I don't need it. I'm fourteen—practically an adult. I don't want some governmental group home leader on my back ordering me around."

"You do not like being told what to do?"

Jack bit down hard. "I can take care of myself."

Draycos cocked his head once, as if studying him, then straightened up again. "How do you survive?" he asked. "Surely you cannot simply take what you need from others."

"Yeah, well, I could," Jack muttered. "Matter of fact, that's mostly what Uncle Virgil and I used to do."

"Pardon?"

Jack hesitated. But as long as he'd gone this far, he might as well lay out the whole ugly story. "Uncle Virgil was a safe-cracker and con man," he said.

"I do not know those terms."

"A safecracker breaks into safes and vaults and takes the things people have stored there," Jack explained, a twinge of conscience poking like a thorn into his side. "A con man uses words and schemes to talk people out of their money."

Draycos's green eyes were gazing at him with an uncomfortable intensity. "You were thieves."

"That's putting it a bit unkindly, sir," Uncle Virge protested.

"Shut up, Uncle Virge," Jack said tiredly. "Yes. We were thieves."

"And your society permits this?"

"Our society tries very hard to stop it," Jack conceded. "But Uncle Virgil was good at what he did, especially the safe-cracker part. One of the real experts in the field. The cops knew all about him, but they never caught him in the act or had enough evidence to arrest him."

"What was your part in his activities?"

"I was his helper," Jack said. "I distracted people, or played foil or backstop. He had me crack some simple safes, too, and he was starting to teach me some of the fancier tricks when he died. I think he was training me to follow in his footsteps."

"Cops," Draycos said thoughtfully, as if finally finding a jigsaw puzzle piece he'd been looking for. "That was the word. You said our attacker on the *Havenseeker* might be a cop. Are the authorities still seeking Uncle Virgil?"

"Actually, they're more likely seeking me," Jack said. "The funny part is that, for once, I didn't do anything."

"Explain."

"I don't steal or con anymore," Jack said. "I never really liked it, and I quit after Uncle Virgil died. But like you said, I have to eat. So I do odd jobs or hire the *Essenay* out for short-range transport work."

"There cannot be very much cargo space aboard this space-craft," Draycos pointed out.

"There's enough for small jobs," Jack said. "Anyway, I was on the Vagran Colony when I heard that Braxton Universis was moving its assembly plant there to Cordolane and needed extra freighters for one-time transport jobs. I applied, they gave me ten sealed crates, and off I went."

"Who is Braxton Universis?"

"It's a what, not a who," Jack told him. "Braxton Universis is one of the biggest megacorporations in the Orion Arm. You know what a megacorporation is?"

"No."

"The *Essenay* is like a normal business," Jack said, waving a hand around him. "That ship of yours, the *Havenseeker*? *That* was like a megacorporation."

"I see," Draycos said. "It is a matter of size."

"Size and power both," Jack said. "Anyway, I spent the next four days on ECHO traveling to Cordolane."

"What is this ECHO?" Draycos asked. "You have mentioned it before."

" 'ECHO' stands for Extra-C Hologic Overdrive," Jack told him, "where 'C' is the symbol for the speed of light. It's the system everyone in the Orion Arm uses to get back and forth between the stars."

"I see," Draycos said. "So you traveled to Cordolane?"

"Right," Jack said. "And when I got there—" he grimaced "—one of the boxes was empty."

The tip of Draycos's tail was making slow circles in the air. "Did you stop along the way?"

Jack shook his head. "I went straight from Vagran to the delivery point on Cordolane."

"Then there are only three possibilities," Draycos said. "The first is that an error has taken place."

"Not a chance," Jack said. "They weighed the crates right beside the *Essenay,* and I stood there and watched them load 'em aboard."

"I see," Draycos said. "Then the second possibility is that this was deliberately arranged to implicate you in theft."

"I'd sure like to know how," Jack said glumly. "I'd also like to know why."

"You said you and Uncle Virgil had cheated others," Draycos reminded him. "Could one of them be seeking revenge?"

"I suppose so," Jack conceded. "But then why not just have me arrested?"

"Maybe they think you still have something valuable stashed away," Uncle Virge put in. "Getting you arrested wouldn't get that back for them."

"But framing me might?" Jack shrugged. "Maybe. I don't know how any of Uncle Virgil's pigeons could have gotten access to sealed Braxton Universis cargo, though. Or how they could pull off this vanishing act, for that matter."

"You are certain the cargo disappeared?" Draycos asked.

"On Vagran, the crate weighed a hundred pounds," Jack said. "On Cordolane, it weighed ten. You said there were three possibilities?"

"Yes," Draycos said. "The third is that you are lying to me."

His long neck seemed to stretch, and even though he was still lying on the dayroom floor he suddenly seemed a lot taller. "You would not lie to me, would you, Jack Morgan?"

Jack swallowed. "This is the truth, Draycos. I swear it."

"That's why the lad can't go shouting your story from the rooftops," Uncle Virge said. "By now, Braxton Universis will have a warrant out for his arrest. With his, shall we say, somewhat checkered history, no one will believe his story about disappearing cargo."

"Ducking local cops isn't that much of a problem," Jack added. "They're usually overworked, and I know how to play them. But Braxton has their own security unit, and they're way better than everything out there except maybe Internos Police."

"What is Internos Police?" Draycos asked.

"That's the overall law enforcement unit of the Internos," Uncle Virge explained. "The Internos itself is the confederation of Earth and the various human colonies. There's also the Orion Trade Association, which includes humans and the thirty-two other intelligent alien species in the Orion Arm. And, of course, each colony and nation has its own government. Makes for quite a patchwork of laws and regulations."

"We can fill him in on local politics later," Jack said. "The point is that even if the local cops don't have time to look for me, Braxton Security does. I barely got off Cordolane ahead of them, and nearly got nailed when I tried to sneak onto Sakklif."

"That's why we were sitting on Iota Klestis when you were attacked," Uncle Virge said. "We wanted some place away from civilization where we could sit back and try to think this out."

"For which I owe you my life," Draycos said, ducking his head in an odd sort of bowing motion. "I thank you."

"Yesterday's thanks are tomorrow's cold porridge," Uncle Virge said with a sniff. "If you really want to show your thanks, you'll help us figure out what happened to the cargo."

"Of course," Draycos said, as if there had never been any doubt. "I intend to do exactly that."

CHAPTER 8

Jack blinked. It was about the last thing he would have expected the dragon to say. "You what?" he asked, just to make sure he'd heard it right.

"I need your assistance to find my attackers, Jack Morgan," Draycos said. "For you to move freely, we must first erase the false accusation against you. Does this not make sense?"

"It makes wonderful sense," Uncle Virge said. "And just how, may I ask, do you propose to do that?"

"We will start at the scene of the crime," Draycos said. "How long will it take to return to the Vagran Colony?"

"Not very," Jack said, touching a switch on the underside of the narrow dayroom table his fizzy-soda was sitting on. Beneath the glass, the surface changed from wood grain to a set of displays and status monitors. "Let's see . . ."

Uncle Virge, naturally, got there first. "At standard cruising speed we can be there in five days," he said. "If we kick up to full power, we can cut that to twenty hours. Very expensive on fuel, though."

"And it's already been over two weeks," Jack added.

"Seems to me that if there were any clues there, they're long gone by now."

"Perhaps," Draycos said. "Perhaps not. All the more reason why we should return as quickly as we can."

"What *won't* be gone is Braxton Security," Uncle Virge pointed out. "If you walk in there, you might have trouble walking out again."

"You said they were moving that operation," Draycos reminded him. "Will they not all be gone?"

"There are bound to be a few still around tying up loose ends," Uncle Virge said.

"Anyway, the cargo was fine when I left there," Jack pointed out.

"It is still the place to start," Draycos said.

"Jack?" Uncle Virge prompted. "It's your decision."

Jack chewed his lower lip. He honestly couldn't see what good it would do them. Still, they had to start somewhere, and Vagran was probably the last place anyone would expect him to show up. "Sure, why not?" he said with a sigh.

"Then it is decided," Draycos said firmly. "We must change course immediately."

"Not so fast, friend," Uncle Virge said. "I seem to remember you saying something about trading secrets; but so far Jack and I have been doing all the talking. It's your turn now."

The tail tip was making slow circles again. A sign of the dragon thinking? "Very well," Draycos said at last. "You know that our ships were attacked and destroyed. What you do not know is that we were only an advance team."

The skin at the back of Jack's neck prickled. "Advance team for what?" he asked carefully.

"For the K'da and Shontine peoples," Draycos said. "Refugees from our war with the Valahgua."

It took Jack three tries to get any words out. "Did anyone know about this?" he asked, trying to sound casual. "I mean, anyone official?"

"In *any* Orion Arm government, Internos or otherwise?" Uncle Virge added.

"We dealt with representatives of a people called the Chitac Nomads," Draycos said. "They assured us that world was not being used, and would be available for purchase."

"Uh-huh," Jack muttered under his breath. "Uncle Virge?"

"I don't know, lad," the other said hesitantly. "On official records, Iota Klestis belongs to the Triost Mining Group. Still, they don't seem to have done anything with it for thirty years or more. I'm afraid I'm not up on current land-use law, so I can't tell you when a claim like that lapses."

"Either way, I doubt the Chitac Nomads had the rights to sell it," Jack concluded. "Typical Chitac stunt."

Draycos had gone rigid, his green eyes shimmering. "Do you say we were cheated?" he demanded, his voice suddenly an octave lower.

"Easy, easy," Jack cautioned, holding out a calming hand as he pushed himself further back in his chair. He hadn't yet seen the dragon get really mad, and he didn't want to start in a cramped dayroom. "The Chitac aren't swindlers, really. They're just a bit . . . uh . . ."

"A bit casual concerning matters of law and regulation?" Uncle Virge offered.

"Yeah, that's it," Jack agreed. "They probably knew about the planet, knew it wasn't being developed, and figured no one wanted it anymore. I'm sure it was all in good faith."

"Their faith is of no value to us," Draycos growled.

"I'm sure something can be worked out," Uncle Virge assured him hastily. "Really. Iota Klestis is in human-claimed space, and the Internos government has always had a soft spot for refugees. How many of you are coming?"

Draycos hesitated, then dipped his head slightly. "Four million K'da and fifteen million Shontine," he said.

Jack whistled softly. "That's a lot of refugees."

Draycos's eyes bored into him. "No," he said quietly. "Not when you consider that there were once a billion K'da and ten billion Shontine."

"Wait a minute," Uncle Virge said. "Are you saying they're *all* coming?"

"All that remain, yes," Draycos said. "Rather than let the Valahgua destroy us, we made the decision to flee from the lands we loved."

His mouth opened slightly, his sharp teeth glittering in the subdued light. "The world where my comrades died was to be our new home."

Jack swallowed hard. No wonder Draycos was scared. "Except that the Valahgua know they're coming."

Draycos's tail twitched. "Yes," he said. "And despite our caution, they have somehow learned our precise destination."

"And now that the advance team has been eliminated?" Uncle Virge asked.

"There is a meeting arranged before the fleet reaches their new home," Draycos said. "I do not know the location. If the advance team does not send an escort to meet them, the refugee leaders will know something is wrong."

An unpleasant chill ran up Jack's back. "But the Valahgua

and their allies have three of your ships now," he said.

"Yes," Draycos said quietly, his eyes looking oddly haunted. "And from the ships, they surely have learned the location of the meeting. They need only mount the Death aboard one of them, and they will be among the refugee ships before the leaders realize their danger."

He lifted his head up again. "And almost within sight of the world where they had hoped to find peace, the K'da and Shontine races will be destroyed."

Jack took a deep breath. "How long before they get here?"

The dragon's tail twitched. "Six Earth months."

For a long minute the dayroom was silent, with only the distant rumbling of the drive in the background. "Okay, I'm convinced," Jack said at last. "As soon as we get to Vagran, we'll go to the Internos liaison office. Someone there can take you to Earth and StarForce headquarters."

Draycos cocked his head. "You will not take me yourself?"

Jack frowned. "I thought you were all hot to get this to someone official," he said. "Riding a government or StarForce agent is the fastest way to do that. Trust me."

"I do trust you," Draycos said. "That is the point."

Jack blinked. "You've lost me."

"I trust you, Jack Morgan," the dragon said. "You have proven yourself to be a friend and ally. I do not yet trust anyone else in this region of space."

Jack opened his mouth; closed it again. "Look, Draycos, I appreciate the vote of confidence," he said. "Really I do. But this is a job for someone who knows what they're doing, not me."

"Tell me then who betrayed us to the Valahgua," Draycos countered. "Was it the Chitac Nomads? Was it the human who then met with us for the actual purchase? Was it the Triost Mining Group? Was it your Internos government itself?"

Jack spread his hands helplessly. "I don't know."

"Nor do I," Draycos said. "Until I do, I cannot afford to trust anyone else."

Jack sighed. "Uncle Virge? Help me out here, will you?"

"Unfortunately, he's got a point, Jack lad," Uncle Virge said. "I vote we go along with him."

Jack made a face. At least until Draycos had helped clear him of the phony theft charge? Was that when Uncle Virge's vote would suddenly change?

Probably. He'd noticed a lot of conniving and persuasion coming out of the *Essenay*'s computer since Uncle Virgil's death. Could the old scoundrel have somehow imprinted it with more than just his speech patterns? "Fine," he said with a sigh. "If that's the way you want it, I'll play along."

Draycos bowed his head again. "In the name of my people, I thank you, Jack Morgan."

"Your people are welcome," Jack said, yawning. "And just call me Jack, okay? Go ahead and change course, Uncle Virge."

"Computing now," Uncle Virge said. "Do you want me to increase speed, too?"

"Might as well," Jack said. "Not much point in saving fuel if I'm going to wind up in prison anyway. Come on, Draycos, let's catch some sleep. You can have Uncle Virgil's old cabin if you want."

"Thank you," Draycos said. He stood up and stretched catlike, his head and forelegs close to the floor, his tail high up in the air. "I would prefer to stay with you."

"Oh—right," Jack said. He'd almost forgotten the dragon's

need to stay close to his host. The whole idea still made his skin crawl a little. "Well, come on then. It's been a long day."

Jack woke suddenly from a dream where a giant gold boulder had rolled down a hill made of smoky dirt and was doing its best to crush him. He opened his eyes, and in the faint light from the display screen he got a glimpse of Draycos's tail as the dragon disappeared silently out his cabin door. "Uncle Virge?" he murmured, glancing at the clock. He'd been asleep for only three hours.

"I'm on him lad," his uncle's voice came back softly. "He's headed for the cockpit."

Jack felt his stomach tighten. Was Draycos planning to hijack the ship? "What's he doing?"

There was a short silence. "Nothing," Uncle Virge said at last. "He looked over the control settings, checked the monitor station, then left. Now he's headed for the galley."

In succession, the dragon visited the galley, the dayroom, Uncle Virgil's old cabin, and the food/water storeroom. Nowhere did he so much as touch anything. He headed into the corridor leading to the aft section of the ship, sniffing at each of the storage lockers along the way, then looked around the small cargo hold.

It wasn't until Draycos was in the engine room that Jack finally caught on. "He's doing a check of the ship," he told Uncle Virge. "Looking around for anything that might be wrong."

"What, he doesn't trust me?" Uncle Virge asked, sounding rather offended. "Besides, how would *he* know if anything was wrong?"

"Don't be so touchy," Jack scolded mildly. "It's probably just natural caution."

"Humph," Uncle Virge said. "Still, I suppose that as long as he doesn't fiddle with anything . . ."

"That's the spirit," Jack said, rolling onto his other side and pulling up the blanket again. "I'm going back to sleep. Wake me if we hit anything."

"Trust me, you'd know," Uncle Virge said dryly.

"Good night, Uncle Virge."

But he didn't fall asleep right away. This thing with Draycos was like the dogs he'd read about once who would prowl around their masters' houses several times a night making sure everything was all right.

Jack had never owned a pet before, but he'd always wondered what it would be like. Maybe this was his chance to find out.

But no. Draycos wasn't a pet. He was a thinking, talking, very independent creature on an important mission. Jack had better not start thinking of him like a trained dog instead of the K'da warrior that he was.

He smiled lopsidedly in the darkness. Not a problem. If today was anything to go by, Draycos would be sure to remind him about that at least once an hour.

A subtle reflection flicked across the bulkhead a few inches in front of his face. "Everything all right?" he called.

"As best as I can tell," Draycos replied. "I am sorry to have awakened you."

"That's okay," Jack said, rolling over again to face the dragon. "You coming back aboard?"

Draycos seemed to study him. "I can stay away awhile longer, if you'd prefer."

"It's up to you," Jack told him, trying not to let his relief show in his voice. This whole thing was still very new, and he wasn't very comfortable with it. The longer the dragon was able to keep his distance, the better.

"Then I will sleep here for the present," Draycos said.

"Okay."

For a few minutes the room was silent. Draycos lay down on the deck in the middle of the room, facing the door like a guard dog on duty. The dragon's golden scales glinted faintly in the light from the display, shimmering whenever he moved. Jack gazed at the shadowy figure, still trying to wrap his mind around all this.

"So how long were you two together?" he asked suddenly.

The long neck lifted and half turned toward him. "Pardon?"

"You and your—what did you call him?"

"My symbiont?"

"Yeah, that. How long were you together?"

The gold-scaled tail flicked slightly. "Polphir and I were companions for ten of your years," the dragon said.

Jack frowned. "Is that Earth years, or something else?"

"It is the unit we were told was your time basis," Draycos said. "Is there more than one form of the unit?"

"No, if they just said years, they meant Earth Standard," Jack confirmed. "You just seem older than that, somehow."

"I am," Draycos said. "Polphir was my second host. I had been with another, named Trachan, for fifteen years before that. And of course I had a guardian host during the five years I was a cub."

"Ah," Jack said. So the K'da was somewhere around thirty. That seemed more reasonable. He wondered if that was considered young or old for their species. "So what happened to Trachan? You two just split up?"

"Shontine and K'da do not 'split up,' " Draycos said stiffly. "He was killed in battle with the Valahgua."

"Oh," Jack said, grimacing. "Sorry. I didn't mean to . . . you know."

"It is all right," Draycos said quietly. "At least I was able to mourn him properly. With Polphir . . . a proper farewell is not yet possible."

"I'm sorry," Jack said again, feeling embarrassed and depressed at the same time. He'd started the conversation in hopes of learning a little more about this strange houseguest they'd picked up. Instead, all he'd accomplished was to dredge up unpleasant memories.

Served him right for starting a conversation in the middle of the night. "I guess I should let you sleep now, huh?" he added lamely.

"And you must be tired, as well," Draycos said.

"Yeah," Jack said. "Well . . . good night."

"Good night."

Taking a deep breath, Jack rolled over and adjusted the pillow beneath his head. There was a lot he still didn't know about these creatures, and a lot he still needed to know. But there would be time for that.

Anyway, the important point was that the dragon had been fed, he'd been talked to, and it seemed safe to be around him. That was enough for now.

Eventually, of course, things would probably get trickier. Things usually did. But as Uncle Virgil had been fond of saying, that was a worry for another day.

Later, when Draycos returned to his back, he didn't even wake up.

CHAPTER 9

It was early evening, local time, when the *Essenay* put down at the main Vagran Colony cargo spaceport.

Or, rather, when the light freighter *Donkey's Age* put down there. Rather than risk bringing the police or Braxton Security down on their heads right from square one, Jack had decided to use a fake ship ident. It was one of a set of four fakes that Uncle Virgil had bought the same time he'd installed the chameleon hull-wrap.

He used a fake ID for himself, too, and got through customs without raising any alarms. A few minutes later he was walking along the high-ceilinged tube that led inward toward the central terminal building. "You're being very quiet," he commented as he walked. "Do I take it a K'da warrior would never do anything so dishonorable as sneaking in under a phony name?"

"The warrior code recognizes that camouflage is often necessary," Draycos said from his right shoulder.

"But you still don't like it."

Draycos hesitated, just enough. "I am still learning the ways of your society," he said.

"In other words, you don't like it," Jack concluded, wondering vaguely why he was even arguing the point. Certainly Draycos didn't want to argue it. Was he actually trying to push the dragon into telling him he'd done something wrong?

If he was, he was wasting his time. "This place is not as I expected," Draycos said, again ducking the question. "Why are there no other beings here? I understood this to be the chief cargo area for this world."

"Doesn't say much for the world, does it?" Jack agreed, giving up the argument. The tube they were walking along was dirty, as if it hadn't been cleaned or even swept in weeks. Embedded in the graytop beneath their feet, the cargo-carrier monorail tracks looked a little rusty, as if they hadn't been used in years. "And I've been to worse places than this, too."

"Yet an important corporation like Braxton Universis had an assembly plant here?"

"Cheap labor, probably," Jack said. "Humans and lots of different aliens, too. There's also tons of raw materials out beyond the settlements. The place hasn't been developed very much."

"They are unfair to their workers?"

"No idea, really," Jack said. "Anyway, the tubes Braxton used are in much better condition. This place is laid out like a lopsided starburst. There's a big three-story warehouse and terminal building in the middle, with all these tubes leading off to the different landing pads. You bring stuff into the warehouse by rail, pass it through customs if you have to, then rail it out these tubes to the ships."

He pointed ahead. "The tube and landing pad I used with the Braxton cargo is on the far side of the warehouse."

"Should you not have landed us closer to it?"

Jack came to an abrupt halt. "Look, pal, if I had enoug[h] money to swim in I wouldn't be in this trouble in the firs[t] place," he growled. "You've already cost me a lot of fuel burning ECHO to this place. Now you want me to pop for the expensive landing pads, too?"

"My apologies," Draycos said. "I did not realize there would be extra cost involved."

"There's always extra cost involved," Jack muttered, starting up again. "Be happy I even got us a pad at the same spaceport."

They continued on in silence, the clunk of Jack's boots on the graytop the only noise. Ahead, the tube widened as it entered the main warehouse building. Jack went in, his footsteps echoing softly now from the distant walls and high ceilings. The middle part of the floor was marked off into different-sized rectangles, with walkways wide enough for loading-carts running between them.

A few of the rectangles were empty, but most were piled with stacks of shipping crates of various sizes and colors. The narrow and rather crooked walkways between the piles made quite a maze. Twenty feet up, catwalks and cranes formed their own maze, some of the walkways connecting with small offices that lined the walls of the second floor. One or two of the office doors were showing lights, but most of the spaceport's staff seemed to have quit for the day. The overhead lights were set at nighttime levels, giving the whole place a rather gloomy air.

The simplest route to the tube they wanted, he knew, would be around the edge of the warehouse. But going that way would mean a longer walk, and Jack was already feeling jumpy about being here. Navigating the maze of boxes would be quicker, and would offer the extra bonus of keeping him out of sight. Picking out a gap between two sets of greenish-brown boxes, he headed toward it.

"Is it always this quiet?" Draycos asked.

"In case you hadn't noticed, it's evening out there," Jack reminded him. "Vagran ports usually aren't busy enough to need a late shift."

He glanced around. No one was visible, but there could easily be groups of workers out of sight in the maze of stacks. "And keep your voice down," he added. "Bad enough to look like I'm talking to myself. I don't want to look like I'm answering back, too."

"I will be more careful," Draycos promised, lowering his voice to a level where Jack could barely hear it himself. "What exactly was the cargo that vanished?"

Away to their left, near the entrance to one of the other tubes, a group of chattering Jantris in maintenance coveralls appeared. "The invoice called it a molecular stress-gauge something-or-other," Jack said, picking up his pace a little and keeping a wary eye on the Jantris. That particular species loved to talk, especially to strangers, and the last thing he wanted was to get trapped into some rambling conversation with them.

The concern turned out to be unnecessary. The Jantris went to the next tunnel around the edge and disappeared down it, still chattering among themselves. Taking one last look around, Jack stepped between the greenish-brown stacks and headed into the maze. "And you saw this device?" Draycos asked.

"Of course not," Jack said impatiently. "I already told you the boxes were sealed. But there was *something* in there. And that something was gone when I got to Cordolane."

"Did the police have any thoughts?"

"If you think I waited around to hear what the cops had to say, you're nuts," Jack said darkly. "I just unloaded the boxes where they'd told me to put them and took off."

"That may have been foolish," Draycos pointed out. "Running creates the appearance of guilt."

Jack snorted. "What kind of appearance does standing there like an idiot with an empty cargo box create?"

"Perhaps you do not understand my question," Draycos persisted.

"You're the one who doesn't understand," Jack retorted. He took a deep breath. "Look. Our law says a person is innocent until proven guilty. Doesn't mean a thing. Uncle Virgil is on their books as a thief, and I fly with Uncle Virgil. They smell even a hint of trouble near me, and they won't stop to wonder if there might be some other explanation. You think I'd be able to prove my innocence from jail?"

"But you told me you have changed your life."

"Sure I have," Jack said bitterly. "But who knows that? No one, that's who. You may not realize this, noble K'da poet-warrior that you are, but it's a lot easier to hang onto a good reputation than it is to tear down a bad one and start over from scratch."

"Perhaps I can assist you with that process," Draycos said.

"Yeah, thanks," Jack said. "I'll settle for you helping me out of this particular mess."

"I will do my best." Draycos's head lifted slightly from the skin of Jack's shoulder, his eye ridges and spiny crest pushing up against the shirt and leather jacket. His tongue flicked out twice. "As to smelling trouble, what is that odor?"

Jack inhaled slowly. There was something in the air, all

right. Faint, but tart and vaguely disgusting. "I don't know," he said, sniffing again. "Doesn't smell like any normal spaceport stuff."

"No," Draycos agreed, his tongue darting out again. "It smells like something dead."

Jack hissed softly between his teeth as the smell suddenly clicked. "You're right," he said. "It's dead meat. Freshly dead meat, in fact."

And where there was freshly dead meat . . .

"Let's get out of here," he muttered, throwing a quick look around as he broke into a jog.

"Is there danger?" Draycos asked, his head rising up farther out of Jack's shoulder.

"Stay down, will you?" Jack growled as he drew his tangler. The extra weight whenever Draycos went three-dimensional always threw him off balance. "Yeah, there's danger. Dead meat means scavengers. *Fresh* dead meat means scavengers who don't mind killing." He reached the edge of a stack of crates and carefully looked around it.

There they were: at least a dozen cat-sized animals with dirty black-and-white speckled fur, ratlike faces, and wicked-looking teeth and claws. Most of them were gathered around an unidentifiable carcass, still chewing away. Others squatted a little ways off, busily grooming themselves after their meal.

The carcass, he noticed with a sick feeling in his stomach, was wearing the remains of a maintenance coverall.

"Heenas," he whispered to Draycos. He backed carefully away from the corner, feeling sweat gathering on his forehead.

There was a sudden weight on his shoulder. He glanced around to find Draycos's head rising up from his back, twisted to look behind them. "Draycos—"

"Behind you!" the dragon snapped.

Jack spun around, the tangler swinging around with him.

Ten feet away, moving silently toward him like miniature lions stalking their prey, were eight more heenas. Their yellow eyes looked impossibly bright in the dim light. Their fur stuck straight out from their bodies, making them look even bigger than they already were. The three in front were already crouching, ready to spring.

Lowering his aim, Jack fired.

The tangler cartridge caught two of the front three heenas in its milky-white threads. The third was too fast, managing to jump sideways out of range. The two trapped animals squealed as the tangler's shock capacitor sparked, putting them out of the fight.

The other heenas, without any sound or reaction, continued toward him.

Jack backed up to the stack of crates, his heart pounding in his ears as he did the math. There were six heenas in front of him, plus the dozen he'd already spotted just around the corner. That made eighteen, plus any more that might be skulking around somewhere else.

Problem was, there were only seven cartridges left in his tangler. He had a spare clip, but he doubted he'd get a chance to use it. The dead maintenance worker was grisly evidence of how fast a pack of heenas could move when they wanted to.

"Do not fire," Draycos said from his shoulder. Jack had just enough time to frown—

And then, with the usual surge of weight, the dragon sprang off his chest and shoulder, shoving aside shirt and jacket as he emerged.

Only this wasn't the nice shiny golden dragon Jack had rescued from the wrecked K'da ship.

This dragon was pure black.

Jack gasped with surprise. Draycos landed on the graytop directly in front of the heenas, his head and forelegs low, his tail arched over his head like a scorpion's. For maybe half a second they all just stood there, the six vicious pack animals and the single K'da warrior facing them. The heenas bared their teeth; Draycos gave a low, warning growl.

As if that was the signal they had been waiting for, the heenas attacked.

The one in the lead leaped directly toward Draycos's snout, its claws extended toward his face. The other five charged toward the dragon's sides, two toward his left and three toward his right, veering wide to keep out of reach of his forelegs. Jack had been right; the heenas were fast.

But Draycos was faster.

The heena going for the dragon's face went first, spinning away with a single startled squeak as Draycos batted it aside in midair with his paw. Even before it disappeared around the side of a stack of crates, the dragon had jumped sideways over the two heenas coming in toward his left, escaping from the center of their encircling maneuver.

They spun around and shifted direction. This time, all five charged him together.

Slashing with his forelegs, moving almost too fast for Jack to see, he batted them away one by one into the gloom.

Jack stood with his back against the stack of crates, his tangler hanging almost forgotten in his hand as he watched Draycos send them flying. His mind flashed back to the leaps the dragon had made aboard the *Havenseeker*, clearly, K'da had tremendous muscular strength.

Draycos was down to his last enemy when the ones that had been feeding around the corner came charging at him, probably alerted by the noise. Two broke off from the pack and veered toward Jack, who snapped out of his paralysis in time to get them with another tangler shot. The rest headed straight for Draycos.

Six-to-one odds had been no contest. It was now quickly apparent that even at twelve to one the heenas didn't have a chance. Draycos waded into the pack, slashing and biting, his tail whipping about with blinding speed and deadly accuracy. Twice it looked to Jack as if they were surely going to overwhelm him, but both times he leaped out of their midst just in time. Landing outside their circle, he continued his slashing attack at the ones on the edge, throwing the whole pack into confusion.

And then, without warning, he leaped straight back toward the stack of crates behind Jack. Automatically, Jack ducked; and as he glanced up, he saw a heena dropping toward him from the top of the stack. Before he could even start to bring up his tangler, Draycos intercepted the attacker, batting it away with his tail.

The dragon's momentum carried him back into the crates, but like a cat he twisted around and got his feet up in time. For a second he hung there on the boxes the way he had from the tree outside his wrecked ship, his brilliant green eyes looking brighter than ever against the black scales. Then, shoving himself off the crates, he landed again on the graytop between Jack and the heenas. Crouching down with his tail raised, he gave another growl.

That was enough for the heenas. Still without a sound, they turned and scattered, scurrying around the stacked crates and vanishing into the dark.

Jack hadn't realized he was holding his breath. Now, he let it out in a huff. "Wow," was all he could think to say.

Draycos's neck twisted around, his eyes searching the shadows for more enemies. Then, slowly, he straightened up and turned back to Jack. "Are you injured?" he asked.

"No," Jack said, gazing at the dragon in fascination. At close range, he could see now that the scales weren't entirely black: the little sliver of red at the edge of each one was still there. "No. I'm fine. Thanks to you."

Draycos cocked his head to the side. "Yet you seem disturbed."

"Just a little sandbagged, that's all," Jack assured him. Was the gold color starting to creep back into the dragon's scales? "You've been calling yourself a warrior; but up to now all I've seen you do is zap people with their own weapons and fire missiles from the *Essenay*'s control board. I didn't know you could fight like *that*."

"A warrior must be adept in all forms of combat," Draycos said.

"I guess so," Jack said. No mistake; Draycos's scales were definitely turning gold again. "That color change is pretty cool, too."

"It is a side effect of K'da combat rage," Draycos told him, lifting up a foreleg to study it. "Our blood is black. As it flows more strongly to our muscles, some of it displaces the color in our scales. Do humans not have a similar danger response?"

"Not really," Jack said. "Well, maybe a little," he corrected himself. "Our faces get hot when we're mad or scared. On some people it shows a little."

"Ah. Interesting."

"Yeah," Jack said, glancing around. "Can we get out of here now?"

"Do not worry." Draycos peered one last time into the shadows, then suddenly turned and leaped. Reflexively, Jack jerked back, whapping his head against the crates. The dragon hit his upper chest above his shirt and melted back onto his skin. "They will not bother us again," he said, sliding along Jack's body until his head was back in its usual place on his right shoulder. "Shall we continue?"

Jack rubbed the back of his head. He was never, *ever* going to get used to this. "Yeah," he said. "Sure."

CHAPTER 10

They reached the far side of the warehouse without any further trouble. "Okay," Jack said, waving a hand around. "This was the pick-up area. What now?"

His answer was a sliding movement along his right arm. Before he could say anything, there was the familiar sudden weight, and Draycos burst from the sleeve of his leather jacket.

Sending an equally sudden flash of pain through Jack's wrist as he left. *"Ow!"* Jack yelped.

The dragon hit the graytop and twisted back around. "What is wrong?" he demanded.

"You almost broke my arm, that's what's wrong," Jack snapped, clutching his wrist where Draycos's emerging bulk had compressed it against his jacket. "Geez."

"I do not understand," Draycos said, stepping close.

"This is leather," Jack said, hooking a finger in the jacket's cuff for the dragon's inspection. "See? Leather. Leather doesn't stretch. This is a snap holding the sleeve cuff together. See? Snaps don't stretch, either."

"I see," Draycos said. "I apologize."

"Yeah, it's okay," Jack muttered. The pain was already starting to fade. "Only the next time you want to go out that way, let me know first, okay? Give me a chance to unsnap it."

"No need," Draycos said, tossing his head in a way that reminded Jack of a horse. "I will not do that again."

"Good enough," Jack said. Beneath the jacket sleeve his shirt felt odd. Popping the snap, he gave it a quick look. Draycos's careless exit hadn't been enough to pop the jacket snap, but it had had no trouble popping the button off the shirt cuff.

"That was my fault, too?" Draycos asked, stretching his long neck to peer at the sleeve.

"Don't worry about it," Jack told him. "I've been on my own long enough to know how to sew on buttons." He shook his head. "I bet I'm the only person in the Orion Arm who needs dog flaps in my wardrobe."

"Pardon?"

"Skip it," Jack said, resnapping the jacket sleeve. "I repeat: what now?"

"We will investigate," Draycos said. He looked around, then padded off.

Jack watched him go, rubbing his wrist as he groused silently to himself. Coming here had been a complete waste of time. He knew it, Uncle Virge knew it, and if Draycos had any brains he'd have known it, too.

So how and why had he let the dragon talk him into this in the first place?

On the other hand, he'd already seen Draycos pull some pretty cool tricks out of his hat. Maybe there really was a chance.

He hoped so. He really did. After all the scams and thefts he'd helped Uncle Virgil pull off, it would be pretty unfair if he had to stay on the run for something he didn't even do.

Speaking of Uncle Virgil . . .

With a sigh, he reached into his inside coat pocket and pulled out the old police EvGa scanner Uncle Virgil had lifted from somewhere a few years ago. Getting his comm clip out of another pocket, he attached it to his shirt collar and turned it on. "Uncle Virge?"

"About time," Uncle Virge said. "What took you so long?"

"We ran into a little trouble," Jack told him, activating the EvGa and keying it to run its data transmissions through the comm clip. "You getting the signal?"

"It's fine," Uncle Virge said. "What sort of trouble? Was it the dragon's fault?"

"Hardly," Jack said. "We ran into a pack of heenas. Draycos was the one who got us out of it."

"I see."

Jack frowned. There was an odd tone in Uncle Virge's voice. "What's that supposed to mean?"

"You should have called," Uncle Virge said. "You should have let me know."

"There wasn't a whole lot of time," Jack pointed out dryly. "Besides, what could you have done?"

"That's not the point," Uncle Virge said. "I don't like you being out of touch with me for so long."

"Hey, *you* were the one who didn't want me transmitting until we had the scanner hooked up," Jack reminded him. "Traceable radio signals, remember?"

"Of course I remember," Uncle Virge said huffily. "I just didn't think you'd take so long to get there."

Jack frowned. "What's gotten into you, anyway?" he demanded. "Come on, let's hear it."

There was a short pause. "What's gotten into me is your

new friend," Uncle Virge said, lowering his voice. "I don't trust him. We know practically nothing about him, you know. Him *or* his people *or* his situation. He could be spinning us a complete rainbow and we'd never know it."

"You mean like the rainbows you're always spinning on me?" Jack couldn't resist pointing out.

"Exactly my point," Uncle Virge agreed. "As the saying goes, it takes one to know one. And you know as well as I do that a con man's first job is to convince the pigeon he's far too good a person to even *think* of doing anything dishonest."

"Uh-huh," Jack said, nodding. He got it now. "It's not so much that you don't trust him. You just don't *like* him."

"You see any reason why I should?" Uncle Virge countered stiffly. "All right, no, I don't like him. I don't like the way he's giving orders and taking charge of everything. I especially don't like the way he keeps trying to fill your head with this warrior-ethic claptrap of his."

"He is not filling my head," Jack protested. "Besides, what's claptrappy about it?"

"You don't think it's claptrappy to risk your life and safety just to keep an enemy from burning his little hands?" Uncle Virge asked pointedly. "Back on Iota Klestis, remember?"

"Well . . . okay, maybe that was a little strange," Jack had to admit. "But—"

"Did it gain you anything?" Uncle Virge persisted. "That's the scale you have to measure everything against, you know. Do you think that thug will be grateful enough to do you a good turn if you ever meet up with him again?"

"Well, no, probably not," Jack had to admit that one, too. "But it didn't hurt us any, either."

Uncle Virge sighed. "That's not the point, Jack lad," he

said. "It could have hurt you a lot. It could have given his friends time to grab you, or to find the ship. But that's not the point, either."

"Then what *is* the point?"

"That this noble K'da warrior bit sounds fine when you read it in a storybook," Uncle Virge said bluntly. "But in real life, it just doesn't work."

Jack looked over at Draycos, prowling along a row of large storage lockers that lined the warehouse wall near the entrance to the tube. "It seems to work okay for Draycos," he said.

"I'm sure it used to," Uncle Virge countered. "It's easy to be grand and noble when you're a soldier, surrounded by lots of other soldiers. It's quite a bit different when you're alone. Did you ever hear of the Dragonbacks?"

Jack frowned. "No."

"They were a small group of idealistic, do-gooder soldiers that came out of Trantson about a hundred fifty years ago," Uncle Virge said. "Each of them had a small dragon tattoo on his back just between his shoulder blades. Said it gave them strength and courage."

"Sounds Chinese," Jack offered. "Dragons were a big deal in their ancient legends."

"Actually, they did claim they were inspired by some obscure Terran Chinese or Japanese story," Uncle Virge said. "Of course, they also said they were descendants of the Knights Templar of Terran Europe, so who knows what they were thinking. If they were thinking at all."

"Sounds like you don't like them."

"What's not to like?" Uncle Virge countered. "The whole group died out maybe ten years after they got started."

Jack puckered his lips. "Because they tried to be helpful?"

"Because they got involved with other people's problems instead of taking care of their own," Uncle Virge said. "That's the lesson here, Jack lad. You have to look out for yourself, because no one will do it for you."

"Jack!" Draycos called.

Jack looked up. The dragon was standing beside one of the lockers about thirty feet away, his head turned in Jack's direction. "Something?" Jack asked.

"Perhaps," Draycos said, his tail twitching. "Come."

Jack was at his side a few seconds later. "What is it?"

"This storage unit," Draycos said, poking his snout at the door. "It is alone of all the others in having this attached to it."

Jack frowned. Stuck across the door beside the lock mechanism was a small sticker with red edges.

A sticker with some very interesting words:

PROPERTY OF BRAXTON UNIVERSIS, INC.

AUTHORIZED PERSONNEL ONLY.

Beneath the words was one of the most recognizable symbols in the Orion Arm: the Braxton Universis corporate logo.

"I do not read your word-symbols," Draycos went on. "What does it say?"

"It says the stuff inside is the property of Braxton Universis," Jack told him. "And that casual snoops like us are to keep our hands off."

Draycos's green eyes glittered. "Yet you said all their material should already be gone."

"Yes, I did, didn't I?" Jack agreed, studying the lock.

"How's it look, lad?" Uncle Virge asked from the comm clip.

"Not too bad," Jack said. The lock was sturdy enough, but it didn't look too complicated. Certainly not for someone who'd studied under Uncle Virgil. "Looks pretty standard for this type of locker. I wish I'd brought some real tools, though."

"What will you do?" Draycos asked.

"We call it breaking and entering," Uncle Virge said, an edge of sarcasm to his voice. "Not something a noble warrior of the K'da would do, I'm sure, but it's better than staring at a locked door and wondering what's inside."

"You said you had a sensor device," Draycos pointed out, gesturing to the EvGa in Jack's hand.

"Sure, but it won't see through locked doors," Jack told him. "It's a police EvGa, an evidence-gathering sensor. It can pull up fingerprints and dust and fiber samples, but not much more than that."

"Then let us first use it," Draycos said. "Afterwards, perhaps there will be another way to look inside."

"Such as?" Uncle Virge asked.

"No, he's right," Jack spoke up quickly. There had been a challenge in Uncle Virge's voice, and he didn't want to sit here listening to the two of them argue. "I'll start with the locker. Ready?"

"Ready," Uncle Virge muttered.

It took five minutes for Jack to run the EvGa over the front of the locker. There were dozens of fingerprints, plus various alien smudges and finger marks. Uncle Virge dutifully logged each one as the sensor picked it up and analyzed it. "A waste of time," he grumbled about every other minute. "A whole army of people could have come through here in the past two weeks."

"Yet this locker warns others to stay away," Draycos pointed out.

"It doesn't say not to touch," Uncle Virge countered. "You almost done, Jack?"

"Finished," Jack said, lifting the EvGa away from the door. "What's the grand total?"

"We've got eighteen separate sets of human prints," Uncle Virge said reluctantly. "There are also finger marks from two different Jantris, three Parprins—"

He broke off. "Three Parprins and . . . ?" Jack prompted.

"Two different Brummgas," Uncle Virge finished, sounding intrigued.

Jack looked at Draycos. The dragon was looking back at him. "Brummgas," he echoed.

"That's right," Uncle Virge confirmed. "Well, well. Small universe, isn't it?"

"Are Brummgas not common among your worlds?" Draycos asked.

"They're common enough," Jack told him, determined not to jump to any conclusions here. "They specialize in low-voltage muscle."

"Pardon?"

"Strong backs, weak minds," Jack explained. "Mercenaries, guards, heavy lifting—that sort of thing. There's no reason to make a connection with the Brummga we ran into on the *Havenseeker*."

"I understand," Draycos said. But he nevertheless sounded thoughtful.

"Can we get on with this?" Uncle Virge suggested.

"Right," Jack said, looking around. Even after hours, someone was bound to wander this direction sooner or later. "We'll do the floor around the locker now."

"You're joking," Uncle Virge protested. "What in the name of buttered toast do you expect to find there? That whole army will have *walked* by, too, you know."

"Scanning now," Jack said, leaning over and holding the scanner a few inches off the floor. "Start recording."

This time, though, Uncle Virge was right. They found nothing interesting, or at least nothing that didn't belong in a spaceport. A whole army *had* apparently walked past the locker.

"At least we've got the fingerprints," Jack said, putting the EvGa away and pulling out his multitool. "Now for the door, I guess. You said there was another way to get in, Draycos?"

"To look in," Draycos corrected. Crouching down, he bounded at Jack's chest and melted onto his skin. "Will you stand with your back pressed against the door?" he added from Jack's shoulder.

Jack frowned sideways down at him. "Tell me first what you've got in mind," he said warily. "You've already torn one of my shirts and nearly broken my wrist."

"There will be no damage," Draycos assured him. "Do you recall my picture of how the K'da can seem to become two-dimensional?"

"That data reader thing you showed me on the *Haven-seeker*?" Jack asked. "Sure. Not that I really understand it."

"It is not an easy concept," Draycos conceded. "But think back to that picture now. This time, imagine that the data reader can bend."

"Hold it," Jack said. "You lost me."

"Use your hand," Draycos suggested. "Hold it flat against your arm."

"Okay," Jack said, holding up his right arm and laying his left hand flat along the forearm. "That's two-dimensional." He angled the hand like a drawbridge going up, leaving the heel of his hand against the arm. "And now it's one-dimensional. Right?"

"Correct," Draycos said, the top of his head poking up off Jack's shoulder again. "Now leave your hand up, but curl your fingers back down to touch your arm."

"Uh-*huh*," Jack said as he did so. "So if there was something between the fingers and the palm—"

"Such as a wall," Uncle Virge put in.

"—such as a wall," Jack agreed, "you'd be leaning over it."

"I'll be dipped in butter and rolled in bread crumbs," Uncle Virge murmured. "You can see through walls."

"Provided the barrier is narrow enough," Draycos said. "Though Jack is correct; we refer to it as seeing 'over' a barrier."

"You can call it orange marmalade if you want to," Uncle Virge said, sounding genuinely enthusiastic for the first time since they'd met Draycos. "Well, well. Now *that's* a talent worth exploring."

"Uncle Virge," Jack warned.

"I know, I know—you're reformed," Uncle Virge soothed him. "But if you *weren't,* imagine the kind of team you two would make."

"We do not use our abilities to steal," Draycos said, sounding offended by the very suggestion.

"Maybe *you* don't," Uncle Virge said. "But I'll bet plenty

of your people have. Or are all K'da so lily-pure that the thought of doing something illegal never even crosses their minds?"

"Of course we are not perfect beings," Draycos said. "But—"

"Can we get on with this?" Jack interrupted, turning his back to the locker and pressing hard against it. "Draycos, do I need to take off my jacket?"

His only answer was another sliding sensation against his skin. He concentrated on the feeling, but couldn't distinguish it from any other time Draycos moved around on him. Maybe sorting out the dragon's moves would come with practice.

For a few seconds nothing happened. Jack kept his back pressed against the locker, fingering his multitool and trying to imagine the kind of jobs Uncle Virgil would have put Draycos to if he'd had the chance.

Of course, convincing a noble K'da warrior to help him break into bank vaults would have been a sizable job all by itself. Certainly would have been an interesting conversation to sit in on.

Maybe he'd still get the chance. There was a lot of Uncle Virgil in Uncle Virge, after all. And if there was one thing Uncle Virgil had always loved, it was a challenge.

"There is a single item in here." Draycos's voice sounded muffled and distant, yet at the same time oddly close. Was the sound transmitting along Jack's back, perhaps? "It is a large cylindrical container, perhaps half your height, with tubing and smaller square boxes attached to its base."

Jack made a face. From that description, it could be practically anything. "Any writing on it?" he asked. "Manufacturer, model name—anything?"

"There are several groups of word-symbols," the near-far answer came. "However, as I have said, I do not know how to read them."

There was another skin-slide, and out of the corner of his eye Jack saw Draycos's head reappear on his shoulder. "However, I could attempt to reproduce it for you, figure by figure," he offered.

Jack shook his head as he stepped away from the locker. "That would take time. And it might still not tell us anything."

He lifted his multitool. "So. I guess we'll have to do this the old-fashioned way."

CHAPTER 11

After Uncle Virge's comment about breaking and entering, he expected Draycos to object to the procedure. But the dragon remained silent as Jack knelt down beside the lock. Maybe this *wasn't* something a noble K'da warrior wouldn't do.

Though only if necessary, of course.

As Jack had already noted, the lock was sturdy but not complicated. He swiveled out one of the blades from his multi-tool, a special gadget Uncle Virgil had spent hours building into one of the tool's original screwdriver heads. This wouldn't take long at all.

He paused, frowning. There was something not quite right about the lock mechanism, he realized suddenly. Not quite symmetric, actually. He leaned closer for a better look, and it was then that he noticed the extra piece of metal extending off the lock about a quarter of an inch to the right. A piece that didn't quite blend in with the original design.

"What is wrong?" Draycos asked, his head rising up from Jack's shoulder.

"The lock's been wired," Jack told him, running his finger by the extra metal strip, being careful not to touch it. "Something's been added to the lock, with this piece of metal there to cover it. Ten to one it's a trip-line."

"What does that mean?"

"It means that if I spring the lock, someone's going to know."

"Interesting," Draycos murmured. "It is not part of the standard lock mechanism?"

"Definitely not," Jack said, shaking his head. "In fact, I don't think I've *ever* seen anything like this on a simple storage locker. Usually if someone wants to protect something, there are better ways to do it."

"Then why was it done?" Draycos asked.

"I'd think that would be obvious," Uncle Virge said tartly. "Even to a noble K'da warrior. They want to know if anyone breaks in."

"But if they are afraid the object inside will be discovered, why not simply remove it from the locker?" Draycos pointed out. "Why leave it inside and then create a trap?"

Uncle Virge snorted. "You familiar with the word 'bait'?"

"I do not know that particular usage," Draycos said calmly. "But from your tone I can deduce its meaning."

"I'm so glad," Uncle Virge growled. "Well, Jack. What now?"

"I don't know," Jack admitted, gazing at the lock. "I can't tell how the trip-line is wired without a scanner and some better tools. And without knowing that, I can't disarm it."

"You have the necessary equipment aboard the *Essenay*?" Draycos asked.

"Sure," Jack grunted. "But I'd never get it in past customs. The Vagran Colony really leans hard on thieves."

"So it's a stalemate." Uncle Virge sounded disgusted.

"Something like that," Jack said. "I guess that leaves us only one option. We open it up, take a quick look, then head for the tall grass before whoever's at the other end of the trip-line gets here."

He waited a moment, hoping one of the others would either try to talk him out of it or have something better to suggest. But both Draycos and Uncle Virge were silent. Taking a deep breath, he lifted the multitool and set to work.

"Easy, lad," Uncle Virge murmured. "Remember your training."

Jack bit at his lip. Yes; remember his training. His training, and his experience, and his methods.

So much for putting the past behind him.

Thirty seconds later, he had the lock sprung.

"Draycos, keep an ear out," he told the dragon as he lifted the latch and pulled the door open. "Let's see what we've got here."

"Well?" Uncle Virge demanded.

"Just like Draycos described it," Jack said, eying the device as he folded his multitool and put it away. "Let's see; there's a plate attached near the bottom that says 'Hamker-Rovski 550.' That ring any bells?"

"Well, well," Uncle Virge said thoughtfully. "It does indeed. A Hamker-Rovski 550 is a low-temperature refrigeration unit."

Jack frowned. "You mean like a food freezer?"

"Colder than that, lad," Uncle Virge said. "Considerably colder."

Jack frowned harder. Then, suddenly, he got it. He got all of it. "Well, well," he said, smiling tightly. "Or did someone just say that?"

"Yes," Uncle Virge said. "But it bears repeating."

"If you have a thought, please speak it," Draycos put in.

"What, the noble K'da warrior doesn't know everything?" Uncle Virge taunted. "How surprising."

The dragon's head rose further out of Jack's shoulder. "I do not claim to know everything," he said, his voice deep and clearly annoyed.

"Take it easy," Jack soothed him, closing the locker and heading back toward the maze of boxes in the center of the warehouse. They'd seen all they needed to, and it was time to make tracks out of here. "Uncle Virge always likes to get places before everyone else. Just ignore him."

The dragon head sank down a little. "Then explain."

"It's really pretty simple," Jack said. "I should have figured it out sooner. I don't know how much chemistry you know, but there are some substances that can go from solid to gas without becoming liquids first. That means they evaporate without leaving any puddles."

"I am aware of that fact."

"Well, one of them happens to be carbon dioxide," Jack said. "Which happens to be one of the waste gasses we exhale when we breathe."

Draycos's head lifted up. "Someone is coming," he said softly. "Three beings. Perhaps the watchers."

"Terrific," Jack muttered, pausing at the edge of one of the stacks and peering carefully around the corner. No one was visible, but if he concentrated he could just hear the footsteps. "Can you tell which direction they're coming from?"

"There," Draycos said, lifting his snout up and out of Jack's jacket and swiveling his head to point back toward the tube area.

"Ha," Jack said, ducking back into the maze of boxes and heading off at an angle. "Looks like they've outsmarted themselves. They figured my ship would be in one of the closer pads, and I'd just walk straight into their arms."

"You think they were waiting for you?" Draycos asked. "You specifically, and not merely someone investigating the cargo disappearance?"

"Who else would care about Jack being in trouble?" Uncle Virge countered scornfully. "Watch yourself, lad. Your friends back there reacted too fast to be any sort of cops I've ever known."

"Braxton Security, then?" Jack asked, picking a new direction through the maze and taking another quick look around before heading off.

"Who else?" Uncle Virge said. "Let me know when you're two minutes away from the ship and I'll start the engines."

"No, leave them off," Jack said quickly. "Whoever they are, they're not going to be stupid enough to miss a ship revving for a liftoff."

"You're certainly not going to try to hide out in a grounded ship," Uncle Virge pointed out.

"You got that right," Jack agreed, breaking into a jog. "We're heading into the city."

"You're *what*? Jack, lad—"

"I'm closing down," Jack said, reaching up and pulling the comm clip off his collar. "I'll talk to you later."

"Jack—"

Uncle Virge's protest was cut off as Jack shut off the clip. "Is there danger in the city?" Draycos asked.

"Probably," Jack said, stuffing the clip into his pocket. "But not as much as there is behind us. They getting any closer?"

He got five more steps before Draycos answered. "They are not following," he said slowly. "I believe they are moving around the edges of the stacks."

"Trying to cut us off," Jack grunted, picking up his pace. "Let's see if we can beat them."

He broke into a flat-out run, hoping his pursuers were making too much noise of their own to hear him. Once, as he rounded one of the stacks, it occurred to him that barreling through a cargo maze infested with heenas might not be the most brilliant thing he'd ever done in his life. He would just have to hope that they'd learned not to mess with the kid in the leather jacket.

The open area around the outer warehouse wall was deserted when he finally emerged from the stacks. "Draycos?" he asked softly, peering across the open area toward the wide doors where the main cargo monorail tracks came into the warehouse. Outside the doors the ground was well lit, with the lights of the city twinkling in the near distance. As far as he could tell, there was no one out there.

"No one is moving nearby," the dragon said, flicking out his tongue. "Nor do I smell anyone close at hand. This is perhaps our best opportunity."

Jack made a face. And if no one was moving or breathing nearby, but a whole bunch of them were waiting outside for him to show up?

Still, if they were, there wasn't a lot he could do about it. Like their escape from Draycos's wrecked ship, all he could do was go for it and hope for the best. "Right," he muttered. "Here goes."

He had been mildly surprised back on Iota Klestis when more of the Brummga's friends hadn't been ready to pounce as he ran for the *Essenay*. He was even more surprised that no one was lurking in the shadows here as he crossed the graytop and ducked through the cargo entrance.

Once, as he ran across the lighted ground outside he thought he heard a shout behind him. But the sound wasn't repeated, and no one shot at him, and a minute later he was outside the range of the lights and into the comforting gloom of night.

Not that darkness alone was going to give him much safety. Darkness and distance, that was the combination he wanted. He passed the fence at the edge of the spaceport and turned down one of the streets heading into the city.

They'd made it six blocks, and Jack had changed streets twice, when Draycos spoke again. "You are saying the box contained nothing except solidified carbon dioxide?"

"You got it," Jack confirmed, pausing a moment to look around. The last turn had put him on a narrow, winding street lined with closely-packed two- and three-story buildings. A few of the buildings had balconies, which the residents seemed to use mostly for storing potted plants. The street itself wasn't very well lit, and the few pedestrians he could see walking along in the distance were too shadowy for him to make out even what species they were.

"I do not understand the purpose."

"You said it yourself, back on the ship," Jack reminded him, continuing down the street. A delicate aroma was drifting through the air from somewhere, reminding him of fresh-baked cinnamon bread. "Someone wanted to frame me. The dry ice—"

"Pardon?"

"Dry ice," Jack repeated. "That's what we call frozen carbon dioxide. The stuff evaporated slowly enough over the four-day trip to Cordolane for the *Essenay*'s air system to handle the extra gas without triggering any alarms."

The cinnamon smell was getting stronger, he noticed. A bakery nearby, maybe? He hoped so. He was starting to get hungry, and it had been a long time since he'd had a good cinnamon roll.

"What is this place?" Draycos asked. "The smells are not those of humans."

"I'm not sure," Jack said. "I've only been here a couple of times, and never to this side of the port. If I'm remembering the map right, it's the Wistawki area."

"Are they friendly to humans?"

Jack shrugged. "I don't think they're *un*friendly, for whatever that's worth. I remember Uncle Virgil conning a couple of them once; they seemed friendly enough. Gullible, too."

There was silence from his shoulder. Jack winced, realizing that last comment had probably offended his companion. He opened his mouth to apologize—

"Behind us," Draycos murmured.

"What?" Jack asked, his apology and rumbling stomach both abruptly forgotten.

"Footsteps," the dragon said. "It is those who sought us in the warehouse."

CHAPTER 12

Jack didn't even bother to ask how in the world the dragon could tell they were the same footsteps. "We'd better hide," he said, picking up his speed as he looked around. No alleyways; no open doors; no bushes or shrubs he could duck behind. He peered ahead, looking for a cross street, but the nearest one was a long ways away.

"Those platforms," Draycos said. "Would one of those do?"

"The plat—? Oh, the balconies." Jack looked up at the nearest one. It stretched across the full length of the second floor, a good six feet above his head. "Sure, they'd do great. Problem is, they're a little high up, and there's no way to climb them."

There was a sudden weight and pulling at the back of his collar, and out of the corner of his eye he caught a glimpse of Draycos leaping out from the back of his neck. "It can be done," the dragon declared as he landed on the ground.

"Are you nuts?" Jack hissed, spinning around. "You want someone to see you?"

"That way," Draycos ordered, jabbing his snout ahead.

"Run to that building. When I say *jump,* you will jump up toward it."

Jack turned, frowning. The indicated building had a balcony, all right, one with enough of a gap between the potted plants for him to lie down in. But it was no lower than any of the other balconies. "I can't jump that high, Draycos," he insisted, turning back. "If you think—"

He broke off. Draycos had moved twenty feet back and was crouched down in the middle of the street like a sprinter getting ready to run.

And in the dim streetlight, he could see that the dragon's gold scales were turning black. "Go," the dragon ordered again. "Run."

Warrior ethic, Uncle Virge's phrase flitted through Jack's mind. What *did* a K'da warrior do, he wondered suddenly, if an underling disobeyed a direct order? That might be something to ask about when this was all over. "Yeah," he managed. "Right." Turning, he took off toward the building as fast as he could run.

He wasn't alone. Draycos's feet were silent in the quiet street, but Jack could hear the dragon's breath rapidly catching up behind him.

He could also hear the faint sound of footsteps now, approaching from the direction they'd just come. They sounded like they were running, too.

Jack clenched his teeth. Directly ahead of him, he suddenly realized, was the building's main door, half hidden in the balcony's shadow. Was *that* what the crazy dragon had in mind? That Jack should slam into the door hard enough to break it down? He opened his mouth to object—

"Jump!" Draycos ordered, his voice sounding nearly as close as if he'd been riding Jack's shoulder. Automatically, Jack obeyed, bending his knees and jumping as hard as he could. Something slammed into his back, two other somethings jammed hard up under his arms—

And to his shock he found himself arcing upward straight at the balcony.

He didn't have time for anything but a startled yelp before the balcony rail caught him just below the tops of his boots, flipping him over toward a headfirst landing.

Draycos, still gripping him under his arms, got there first. He rolled around beneath Jack as they fell, taking the full brunt of Jack's weight on himself as they sprawled onto the balcony.

"Quiet—they approach," Draycos whispered into his ear. "Down, and behind me."

Jack rolled off onto the dragon's far side, too winded by their landing to say anything. The footsteps were much closer now, and definitely running. Pulling his knees to his chest, rubbing his shins under the tops of his boots where the railing had hit them, he clamped his teeth together hard and lay still. Behind him, he felt Draycos curl around his back, protecting him from view from the street.

The footsteps came to a point just beneath the balcony and faltered to a halt. "What the frunge?" a human voice said quietly. "Where'd the little blinker go?"

"I don't like this," a second human voice growled. "He wasn't *that* far ahead of us."

"Maybe he picked a lock and went inside somewhere," the first voice suggested. "He's supposed to be good at that."

There was a deep snort. "What, into a Wistawki house?"

an equally deep voice demanded. Too deep for human vocal cords, Jack decided. "In this neighborhood? Today? He's not *that* stupid."

"Hey, the kid just got here," First Voice said. "He wouldn't know."

From the distance came a faint roar. Carefully, Jack turned his head just enough to see the sky behind him. There, at the corner of his vision, he spotted the familiar sight of a starship shooting up toward the clouds.

A familiar sight, and an all-too-familiar engine pitch.

"Oh, frunge," First Voice said disgustedly. "There goes the uncle. Looks like your buddies muffed it."

There was a dark-sounding rumbling noise. Jack frowned. He'd heard that sound before.

Abruptly, it clicked. *A bass drum being attacked by a bunch of chipmunks.* Apparently, he and Draycos had run into another Brummga.

"They have not *muffed* it, Drabs," the Brummga ground out. "If the uncle escaped, it is because *your* people failed *their* job."

"Yeah?" First Voice—Drabs—retorted. "Well, if your group—"

"Both of you shut up," Second Voice cut them off. "Forget the uncle. As long as we have the kid, he'll come when he's called."

"Except that we haven't *got* the kid," Drabs pointed out.

"We'll get him," Second Voice promised, and there was something in his tone that made Jack shiver. "Don't you worry about *that.*"

"Perhaps the great Lieutenant Raven knows what we do

not," the Brummga rumbled sarcastically. "Tell us what you know, Lieutenant Raven."

"Watch your mouth, Brummy," Drabs warned. "You people work for us, not the other way around."

"For starters, I know he didn't sprout wings and fly away," Second Voice—Raven—said. "What about those balconies? Drabs?"

"Already checked 'em out," Drabs said. "Nothing that could possibly be human on any of them. Anyway, he'd have needed a jet pack to get up there."

"Then he's still ahead of us," Raven concluded. "Move out, and make sure he doesn't go to ground."

The footsteps resumed, continuing down the street. Carefully, Jack turned onto his back, easing his head up just enough to see over Draycos's side. The two men and their lumbering Brummgan companion were hurrying away down the street, looking right and left to check out possible hiding places.

One of the men, he saw, had an infrared scanner strapped over one eye. All three of them were wearing holstered guns at their sides.

Jack eased back down again, listening to the footsteps fade away into the city noises. "Good thing they've never seen a K'da before," he whispered. "I wonder what you look like on an infrared scanner."

"I do not know," Draycos whispered back. "Are you injured?"

"Not enough to worry about," Jack assured him. In point of fact, his shins were throbbing, and would probably ache for at least a couple more days. Compared to possibly getting shot, it didn't seem worth mentioning.

"I did not intend to miss with the jump," Draycos said. "I apologize."

"It's okay," Jack said. "The boots absorbed most of the impact. I'm still surprised you were able to jump this high with a hundred-odd pounds of Jack Morgan weighing you down."

"I am relieved that it was successful," Draycos said. "Still, I regret my error."

"I said forget it," Jack said impatiently. The sort of people he and Uncle Virgil usually hung around with never apologized even once, let alone twice. The dragon's groveling was making him feel uncomfortable. "Hey, no hospital, no foul."

"Pardon?"

"Skip it." Jack took a deep breath. "So they *were* waiting for me. *And* for Uncle Virgil."

"So it would seem," Draycos agreed. "How is it they do not know he is dead?"

"We didn't exactly announce it to the news nets," Jack said. "Matter of fact, we kept it as quiet as possible. I already told you why."

"Yes; the ownership of your spacecraft," Draycos said. "That point does not appear to apply any longer."

"And that might be a problem," Jack admitted, gazing up at the clouds drifting across the stars. There was nothing to see—Uncle Virge and the *Essenay* were long gone. "They must have been trying to break into the ship," he said. "That's the only reason Uncle Virge would have cut and run."

"Will he simply abandon you?"

Jack shrugged. "We have a standard plan for situations like this," he said. "He'll try first to sneak back into one of the smaller spaceports on Vagran and wait for me. If I don't show, or if he can't get back in without attracting attention, he'll go to a rendezvous spot on another planet and wait for me there."

"That assumes we will be able to get off this world."

"Normally that wouldn't be a problem," Jack said. "There are regular passenger shuttles, and there's always a way to make enough money for a ticket." He grimaced. "Of course, with Lieutenant Raven on our trail it might not be that easy. I wonder what he's a lieutenant of."

For a minute they lay together in silence. "They expected your return," Draycos said at last. "That would mean they are involved with the falsified theft. Perhaps we should try to learn more about them."

"What, you mean go looking for them?" Jack snorted. "At three to one odds? You must be joking."

"The correct ratio is three to two," Draycos corrected him. "You have forgotten about me."

"Hardly," Jack said, carefully sitting up. There was no sign of Raven and his buddies anywhere he could see. "*You* were the one on our side I was counting."

"Ah," Draycos said, uncurling himself. "I see."

"Right," Jack said. "Come on, let's get out of here."

"Sooo soooon?" a slurred and raspy voice came from the corner of the balcony.

Jack froze halfway to his feet. There, sitting against the rail in the shadow between two huge potted plants, was the thin figure of a Wistawk. "Sorry," Jack apologized. "We didn't mean to intrude."

"Not at all," the Wistawk said, getting to his feet like a collapsible ruler unfolding. He wobbled for a moment as if trying to get back on balance, then abruptly straightened to stand perfectly upright. "Come," he said, darting suddenly to the edge of the balcony to stand between Jack and the rail. "Come inside. Join the festivities."

"Ah . . . thanks," Jack said, trying to ease his way past their would-be host. The Wistawk clearly was drunk, and in his state probably thought Jack was another of his species.

Whoever was inside, though, probably wouldn't make that mistake. The Brummga's earlier comment about only a fool trying to sneak into a house in this neighborhood flitted through his mind. Had there been some sort of trouble between humans and Wistawki on Vagran today?

The Wistawk was too fast for them. Moving like a large four-limbed insect, he again got between Jack and any chance of escape. Dimly, Jack wondered how fast the alien would be able to move if he *wasn't* drunk. "Come inside," he repeated. "Preenoffneoff!"

Jack winced as, behind him, the balcony doors were flung open. "Ah, Preenoffneoff!" the drunk Wistawk greeted the newcomer. "Another guest! Welcome him!"

"Another guest?" the newcomer said. His voice, as near as Jack could tell, was stone-cold sober. "What is the meaning of this?"

Slowly, Jack turned around. Another Wistawk, even taller and thinner than the drunk, was standing in the doorway. His arms were folded, and he was staring at Jack with an unreadable expression. In the room behind him were at least twenty more of the aliens, seated in concentric circles around a pair sitting by a fireplace in the center. All were dressed in glittering finery, with ornate headpieces that caught the candlelight and scattered it around the room. All had apparently stopped what they were doing and were looking toward the balcony.

And with a sinking feeling in his stomach, Jack realized what they had done.

He and Draycos had just crashed a Wistawki bonding ceremony.

CHAPTER 13

"Shall we leave?" Draycos murmured from beside him.

"No," Jack muttered back. He'd already seen how fast a drunk Wistawk could move. The group inside didn't seem likely to be that handicapped, which meant that outrunning them was out of the question. Now, too late, he remembered that the Wistawki he and Uncle Virgil had conned all those years ago had been rather elderly. Maybe that was the only reason the two of them had made it out of that scam alive.

Preenoffneoff took a long step out onto the balcony. "Who are you?" he demanded, his voice sounding like sticks clattering together.

Did that mean he was getting angry? Jack wished he knew. "Who am I?" he echoed, stalling for time as he tried desperately to remember something—anything—about bonding ceremonies. Uncle Virgil had had him read up on Wistawki culture in general for that scam, but this particular subject hadn't really come up.

They were sort of like human weddings, he vaguely remembered, but a lot more rowdy. One of the articles he'd read had compared them to a combination of wedding, pie-eating contest, and carnival. They also usually covered a two- or three-block area, with all of the happy couple's neighbors involved in the ceremonies in some way.

No wonder the Brummga had scoffed at the idea of Jack being able to disappear into this neighborhood. If they got mad at him crashing their party, there would be an awful lot of Wistawki he would have to run through before he reached someplace safe.

But even as that depressing thought occurred to him, the key word clicked.

Carnival!

"Who am I?" Jack repeated, drawing himself up to his full height. "Why, I'm one of the entertainers, of course. The Great Jack O'Lantern, here to amaze and enchant and astound the young ones. I trust I'm not late?"

Preenoffneoff had been starting to take another step toward them. Now, though, he paused. "I didn't hire any humans," he said.

"Not specifically," Jack said. "The agency sent me over."

He reached down and patted Draycos's head. "Jack O'Lantern and his amazing electromechanical assistant Draycos." He frowned. "Surely you've heard of us. The Skyway Pavilion on Scintrell? I was one of the star performers there only three years ago."

"There are so many," Preenoffneoff said, waving a hand in a vague gesture as he stepped to one side. "Very well. Come inside."

"Thank you," Jack said, bowing from the waist. "A moment while I get Draycos reset."

He leaned over and reached under Draycos's neck. "I hope you know what you are doing," Draycos murmured.

"Me, too," Jack whispered. "Just play off my cues, and remember you're supposed to be a mechanical robot. Can you sing or dance or anything?"

Draycos turned his head slightly to gaze directly into Jack's eyes. Jack swallowed; those green eyes did not look very friendly at the moment. "Dance?" he repeated ominously.

"No, no, of course not," Jack said hastily. "That's okay, we'll skip the dance."

"Are you ready?" Preenoffneoff asked.

"Ready, willing, and able," Jack said, straightening up. "Lead the way."

The Wistawk turned and walked back into the room. Putting on his most confident smile, Jack followed.

"The whelps are there," Preenoffneoff said, pointing to the outer circle, a ring of short Wistawki Jack hadn't been able to see from the balcony. "We will see your performance now."

"Certainly," Jack said, forcing his smile to stay in place as he felt sweat gathering on his forehead. He had assumed the youngsters would be off in another room somewhere, away from the main festivities. Clearly, the carnival atmosphere was for the adults, too.

Which meant a bigger audience. A more discerning audience. An audience that might decide to tear him into pieces if they didn't like the show.

Terrific.

"Good evening, all," he said cheerfully, bowing to the room in general. "My name is Jack O'Lantern, and this is my amazing electromechanical assistant Draycos. Say hello to the folks, Draycos."

Draycos drew himself up, as if he was going to refuse to play along with this charade. Jack held his breath. . . .

The dragon dropped his head and neck nearly to the floor in a stylized bow of his own, his tail arching up over his head. "Good evening, all," he said.

Holding the pose, he fluttered the tip of his tail as if waving. "And a special good evening to the whelps," he added.

There was an almost human giggle from the outer circle, and Jack started to breathe again. "That's Draycos," he said as Draycos straightened up. "Did I mention he's my amazing electromechanical assistant?"

"Yes," one of the whelps obligingly called.

"He looks real," one of the others added.

"Of course he's real," Jack said. "A real robot. Maybe later, if you're good, I'll let one of you push some of his buttons."

"Me!" the first whelp yipped.

"No, me!" someone else insisted.

"Later," Jack reminded them. "Don't worry, there's enough of him to go around."

There was just the hint of a growl from Draycos, but the dragon didn't say anything. "Now, I need someone to go find me a few things," Jack continued, stepping over to the refreshment table set out along the wall beside the door to the balcony. One of the serving plates was loaded with raw fruits and vegetables. "I'll need a deck of ordinary playing cards, three opaque cups—those are cups you can't see through—and some string or thin rope. And three coins, any size."

"I'll get the cards!" one of the whelps said, scrambling to his feet. Two others were right behind him, scattering to different parts of the house.

"You do not have your own equipment?" Preenoffneoff asked.

"I have my amazing electromechanical assistant Draycos,"

Jack reminded him. He reached to the fruit plate and selected an apple, a pear-shaped white fruit, and a polka-dotted thing the size and shape of a small zucchini. "For everything else, I prefer to borrow from my audience."

He smiled out at the crowd. "After all, anyone can do tricks with special cards, can't they?"

"Show us some tricks!" one of the whelps called impatiently.

"Gee, I don't know if I can," Jack said with mock uncertainly. He stepped away from the table and tossed the apple up into the air. The zucchini followed, and then the pear, then the apple again. It had been a long time since he'd juggled, but apparently the skill hadn't gone rusty. "Maybe you can help me think of some," he added.

Someone giggled. Jack tried varying the pattern a little; someone giggled again. He stole a glance away from the flying fruit, wondering what he was doing that was so funny.

The audience wasn't looking at him. They were looking *behind* him.

And all the children were giggling now.

Carefully, keeping his eyes mostly on his juggling, Jack threw a quick glance to each side. Preenoffneoff was nowhere to be seen. Could he be coming up behind Jack? With a serving knife from the table, maybe?

A drop of sweat trickled down his back. He hadn't been invited here, after all. He'd crashed this ceremony, and there were plenty of species in the Orion Arm who would consider that a good enough reason to cut such an intruder into fish food. Some of those species might even laugh and applaud and giggle while it was being done.

Did the Wistawki think that way? He didn't have the foggiest idea. More to the point, did Preenoffneoff think that way? He didn't know that, either.

All he knew was that the giggling was getting louder, and that the adults were smiling, too. Keeping the fruit in the air, wondering how fast he could go for his tangler if he had to, he turned his head quickly to the right.

It wasn't far enough to see what was behind him. But it *was* far enough to spot Preenoffneoff standing by the balcony door. He wasn't moving toward Jack, and there was certainly no knife or other weapon in his hand. And like the other adults, he was smiling.

Jack focused back on his juggling, thoroughly confused now. Could there be another Wistawk back there? The drunk from the balcony, maybe? Probably not.

Then how about a Wistawk sneaking up on him from the left?

That was possible. Again, Jack twisted his head quickly to the side, this time to his left.

Again, it wasn't far enough to see directly behind him. But again, there was no threat anywhere that direction that he could see.

So what *were* they all giggling at?

He'd tried to play it subtle; but there was nothing for it now but to go obvious. Slowly, still keeping the fruit circling through the air in front of him, he turned around.

Draycos was lying on his back on the floor between Jack and the table, his neck and tail curled upward like a mismatched set of parentheses, busily juggling five of the apples back and forth between his four paws.

Jack let out a quiet huff of relief. So no one was trying to murder him, after all.

A second later, the relief vanished, rolled over by a flood of annoyance. What did Draycos think he was doing, upstaging him that way? How *dare* he?

He let his hands come to a halt, catching the pieces of fruit as they fell, and stood there glaring at the dragon. What was he going to do, he wondered desperately, now that Draycos had ruined his act?

Draycos kept juggling another couple of seconds, then suddenly seemed to realize that Jack was watching him. Letting out a guilty squeak, he quickly stopped, catching one of the apples in each paw.

The fifth apple was still soaring high overhead. Arching his neck, he caught it neatly in his teeth.

Behind Jack came a clatter of the finger-snapping that was the Wistawki version of applause. Draycos held his pose, blinking at Jack like a kid caught raiding the cookie jar.

Slowly, almost reluctantly, Jack realized the dragon hadn't ruined the act at all. In fact, he'd made it far better than anything Jack could ever have come up with on his own.

With a flourish, he turned back to face the Wistawki. "My amazing electromechanical assistant Draycos," he announced, waving a hand back at Draycos. He stepped back to the table and returned his borrowed fruit to the plate, then turned to Draycos and gave a slight nod.

Draycos understood. One at a time, in rapid succession, he tossed Jack the apples he was holding in his paws. Jack caught each in his left hand, tossed it in turn to his right hand and set it back on the plate.

Last, Draycos spat him the fifth apple. Jack caught it and stopped, reacting as if it was wet with saliva. He looked closely at it, made an exaggerated yucky face that got him more giggles from the whelps, and tossed it back to Draycos. The dragon caught it in his mouth, bounced it around to each of his paws, then tossed it back to his mouth. A flash of sharp teeth, and the apple was gone.

"My amazing electromechanical assistant Draycos must have skipped lunch," Jack said dryly over the finger-snapping applause. "Now, who's got that deck of cards?"

CHAPTER 14

The show, in Jack's humble opinion, was a smashing success.

He'd never done a real magic show before, but it was almost as if his whole life had been spent training for one. Most of the tricks he performed were ones Uncle Virgil had taught him, either for scamming money on the streets when he was a little kid, or more recently as distractions for cons the two of them had worked together. Uncle Virgil had taught him sleight of hand, too, both for use in scams and also as dexterity exercises for his safecracking and pickpocket training.

And of course, the glib patter nearly every magician used to talk up the audience was pure con artist. It was like he was back to his old life again. Almost as if he'd never left it.

The only difference was that this time the audience would be giving him money voluntarily instead of him stealing it from them. When Uncle Virge had urged him to remember his training, this probably wasn't what he'd had in mind.

Still, the biggest surprise of the evening, at least to him, was Draycos. From that first bit of scene-stealing juggling, the dragon slid naturally into the role of the magician's smart-alecky assistant.

He played the role beautifully, too. Even when Jack's tricks weren't all that impressive, Draycos's inspired clowning in the background more than made up for it.

It was the last thing he would have expected from a dignified, noble warrior of the K'da. Uncle Virge would never believe it.

They ran the show for nearly an hour before Jack decided it was time for the grand finale. By this time, hopefully, Raven would have moved the search for him to some other part of the city. Depending on what the Wistawki paid for the show, he and Draycos ought to be able to hire a transport to get them to the backwater spaceport on Aldershot where the *Essenay* would hopefully be waiting for them.

"And now, my friends, one final bit of magic for your amusement," Jack told them, slipping off his jacket and holding it out in front of him. "An ordinary coat, as you can see."

He flipped it around, letting them see both the inside and the outside. "I will now ask my amazing electromechanical assistant Draycos to come stand in front of me," he went on, hanging the jacket spread out in front of him in a two-handed grip.

Obediently, Draycos stepped in front of him, staying behind the jacket. Hopping up on his hind legs, he stretched his body up between Jack's outstretched arms, resting his front paws on the top of the jacket. Jack couldn't see what he was doing with his face as he peered over the jacket, but the whelps were giggling again.

"I thank you for your time and your attention and your courtesy," he said, bowing to the room. The movement made the jacket bob up and down; Draycos bobbed right along with it. "Unfortunately," he continued in a sterner voice, "I can't say as much for my amazing electromechanical assistant Draycos. Draycos, you have been decidedly disrespectful to me tonight."

Draycos leaned his head straight back so that his face was upside down to Jack's. "I?" he asked.

"Yes, you," Jack said firmly. "And that last trick was the final straw. I'm afraid I'm going to have to fire you."

There were yips of protest from the whelps. "No, no, I've made up my mind," Jack told them. "Draycos can no longer be my assistant. And when a magician fires an assistant, where do you suppose that assistant goes?"

He let the whelps shout a few possibilities. As they did so, Draycos slid his right front paw along the top of the jacket to rest on Jack's hand. He was onto the plan, all right. "Nope," Jack said shaking his head at the whelps. "As a matter of fact, when a magician fires his assistant, he goes into thin air!"

With a twist of his wrist, he flipped the coat over the top of Draycos's head. There was a brief surge of weight on his right forearm—

He let go of the jacket, letting it drop empty to the floor.

The whelps gasped. For another second there was stunned silence; and then, to Jack's relief, came the loudest burst of Wistawki applause yet. "Once again, my friends, I thank you," Jack said over the finger-snapping, bowing low three times. On his third bow, he retrieved the jacket from the floor.

Preenoffneoff was waiting for him at the door leading from the room. "An impressive show," the Wistawk said quietly. "Fully as impressive as if you had been invited."

"What do you mean?" Jack asked, trying to sound puzzled,

his heart starting to speed up. After knocking himself out for an hour up there, surely Preenoffneoff wasn't going to make trouble for him. Was he?

"You came to our balcony to hide," Preenoffneoff said. "Don't deny it. Randorneoff told me."

Jack felt his heart sink. He'd seen the drunk Wistawk come in from the balcony half an hour ago, but he hadn't realized he'd talked to anyone. He was in trouble, all right. "Well . . ." he stalled, searching frantically for something to say.

"I trust you are safe now?"

It took Jack a moment to change mental gears. "I hope so, yes. And I apologize for breaking into your home."

The Wistawk waved the words away. "An impressive show," he said again, pressing a small velvet pouch into Jack's hand. "Go in peace and merriment."

"Thank you," Jack said, bowing again as he fingered the pouch. It was heavy, and the contents clinked slightly as he shifted them. High-value coins, he hoped. "May your family rest in joy and contentment."

The evening mealtime had passed while they were inside entertaining the Wistawki, and more pedestrians had now appeared strolling the streets. Not surprisingly, most of them were Wistawki, chattering together as they enjoyed the night air. Picking a direction leading away from the spaceport, Jack headed out, keeping to the shadows as much as he could without looking obvious about it.

"Where are we going?" Draycos asked softly from his shoulder.

"There's a small airfield south the city," Jack said. "Hopefully, we now have enough money to hire a plane."

"Where will the *Essenay* will be waiting?"

"At a regional spaceport about half a continent away," Jack told him. "If Uncle Virge wasn't able to sneak back in under a different ID, he'll have gone on to a planet called Aldershot. In that case, I'll have to find a job somewhere until I can make enough money to get us there."

"Perhaps you should continue as a performer," Draycos suggested. "I was quite impressed by your skill."

"Thanks, but I'll stick with something simpler," Jack said dryly. "Like maybe heavy load lifting. Keeping an audience on the hook that way is a little too much like what I used to do."

He glanced down at his shoulder. "Speaking of which, you did pretty good yourself. Especially the juggling. When did you learn to do that?"

"When I was young," Draycos said. "It was a skill my older brother had, and which I very much wanted to master.

"No kidding," Jack said, feeling a twinge of the emptiness he'd always felt when someone mentioned brothers or sisters. "How many brothers do you have?"

"I had just the one brother," Draycos said. "I also have three sisters."

"Big family," Jack said. "Me, I was an only child. So he taught you how to juggle, huh?"

"He assisted, but I mainly taught myself," the dragon said. "I wished to surprise and impress him."

"I'll bet you did," Jack said. "You're darn good at it."

"Thank you," Draycos said. "It is odd, though, for I have always thought of it merely as a private amusement. I would never have expected it to prove a useful skill."

"Sort of backwards from me," Jack said. "Everything I did back there I learned for scamming or stealing or conning. *I* never thought it would be a way to just amuse people."

They walked in silence for another block. "It does not seem to me that your people have much of a childhood," Draycos said at last.

Jack sighed. "My people do all right," he said. "It's me who hasn't had much of a childhood. My parents died when I was three. Some sort of mining accident, I guess."

"You guess? You do not know?"

"I was only three," Jack repeated patiently. "I remember them wearing some kind of funny hats, and I remember that there was a big explosion. But that's about it. I wouldn't even know they'd been miners if Uncle Virgil hadn't told me."

"He told you this after he had adopted you?"

"Sort of adopted me, anyway," Jack corrected. "As far as I know, there was never anything formal about it. He came in after the accident and brought me to live aboard his ship."

"As his assistant in dishonesty."

"Mostly," Jack admitted. "Don't get me wrong. He was all the family I had, and he took care of me. And I do mostly miss him. But . . . yeah, mostly I was just his assistant."

"I am sorry for your misfortune."

"Save it," Jack bit out. He wasn't used to apologies, and he sure wasn't used to people feeling sorry for him. "I don't need your sympathy."

"And you also do not need anyone else?"

"I did all right before you got here," Jack said stubbornly. "I'll do all right long after you're gone, too."

"When I am gone?"

"Skip it," Jack growled. Now that they'd solved the problem of the missing cargo, Uncle Virge would probably push for him to dump Draycos off on someone else for this Valahgua hunting expedition of his. But he hadn't intended to let that slip to Draycos. "So where's this brother of yours? Coming in with that big fleet?"

"My sisters are with the fleet," Draycos said quietly. "But my brother is gone. He died in battle against the Valahgua."

Jack grimaced. "Oh. Sorry."

"There is no need to apologize," Draycos assured him. "It was long ago, and he was properly mourned."

"Mm," Jack said, not knowing what else to say. "So I guess you wanting to save the fleet isn't just your job as a warrior. It's also something personal."

The dragon shifted slightly against his skin. "The K'da and Shontine are my people," he said, "and I would willingly die in the defense of any one of them. But yes, it is also personal."

Jack grimaced. And would he also willingly give his current companion's life to defend these umpteen million people of his? That was something he really ought to get nailed down before they went much farther with this whole thing.

He was trying to think of a polite way to phrase the question when a shadow detached itself from a nearby wall and jammed a gun into the side of his neck.

"Nice and cool, now, Morgan," a familiar voice breathed in his ear.

Jack felt his throat go rigid. Oh, *no*. "Why, Lieutenant Raven," he said as casually as he could manage. "Nice to see you again."

"The feeling is mutual," Raven said. "Now. We can do this the easy way, or we can do it the hard way. Your choice."

Under his shirt, Jack could feel Draycos sliding into position for a leap. "Uh-uh," Jack warned under his breath.

"Uh-uh what?" Raven demanded. "Uh-uh to the easy way?"

"No, just plain uh-uh," Jack said. Draycos subsided; clearly, he'd gotten the message. Though on second thought, maybe he should just let the dragon deal with it his own way.

A second later, he was glad he'd held Draycos back. Halfway down the block, two more shadows pushed away from different walls, one of them the wide bulk of Raven's pet Brummga. Even Draycos couldn't have taken all three of them, not with them spread out that way.

"So the little blinker *did* find a hole to hide in, huh?" Drabs sneered as they converged on Jack and Raven. "Good little blinker."

"You're in a mess of trouble, Morgan," Raven said, reaching around Jack's left side and removing the tangler from its holster. "You know that?"

"Grand theft," Drabs said, still sneering. "That molecular stress-gauge transducer you stole was worth three million dollars."

"Wow," Jack said, letting his mouth drop open in feigned astonishment. "That old white stuff's *really* getting expensive."

Drabs frowned. "What old white stuff?"

"Dry ice," Jack said blandly. "Imagine ninety pounds being worth a whole three million."

The expression that spread across Drabs's face was priceless. "Hey," he said. "Lieutenant?"

"He has solved it," the Brummga rumbled in disgust. "I said that he would."

"Yes, yes, you were brilliant," Raven said, sounding as disgusted as the Brummga. He jabbed his gun again into Jack's neck. "Clever little blinker, aren't you?"

"I try," Jack said modestly.

"And the uncle's gone," Drabs pointed out, starting to sound worried. "What do we do now?"

"What do we do now?" Raven echoed. "We find something else to pin him to the floor with, that's what."

"Such as?"

Raven stepped close behind Jack and looped his left arm around Jack's throat. He turned around, forcing Jack to turn with him.

Coming toward them on the street, chattering together and paying no attention to the strangers in front of them, were a pair of Wistawki. Tightening his left arm, Raven took his gun away from Jack's neck.

Resting his arm on Jack's shoulder, he leveled the weapon at the approaching aliens.

Jack inhaled sharply, suddenly realizing what Raven intended. Ignoring the pressure on his throat, he grabbed for the gun with both hands.

But he was a split-second eternity too late. Raven's gun spat a flash of laser fire, shifted aim slightly, and spat another one.

Without a sound, not even a final yelp, the two Wistawki crumpled to the ground.

"Like maybe a murder," Raven said calmly.

"Are you *insane*?" Jack gasped, staring in horror at the dead Wistawki. "What—why did you—?"

"What's the problem?" Raven said, waving the laser casually beside Jack's face. The barrel radiated heat, and the slight smell of ozone crinkled his nose. "A couple of aliens. No big deal."

"You're insane," Jack breathed. His whole body was starting to shake now, tears were welling up in his eyes, and his stomach wanted desperately to be sick. Never, ever, in all his years of stealing and cheating people had he ever seen someone gunned down in cold blood that way.

"Not me, friend," Raven said. "You're the one who shot them. Right, Drabs?"

"Right," Drabs agreed. He stepped in front of Jack, back to sneering again. "Typical alien-hating human, I guess."

Jack blinked the tears out of his eyes. He would not let these thugs see him cry. He would *not*.

"But we'll talk about all that later," Raven said. "Meanwhile, pleasant dreams."

Something cold touched Jack's neck just above where Raven was still holding him. There was a whiff of something unpleasant. . . .

The last thing he saw was Drabs's face. Still sneering.

CHAPTER 15

The Brummga took charge of Jack, holding the sleeping boy upright with one of his massive arms around his waist. Raven went through his pockets, taking the comm clip, the multitool, and the police EvGa scanner. Then, with Raven walking ahead at point and Drabs lagging behind in rearguard position, they headed back toward the spaceport.

Leaving Draycos still resting unnoticed against Jack's skin, fuming quietly to himself.

He should have acted sooner. He should have acted, period. He should have ignored Jack's warning to remain quiet when Raven first appeared on the scene. A leap from the shoulder would have knocked Raven's gun away from Jack's neck, and it would have been the work of half a second to deal with the human.

But then Raven's two companions would have opened fire from their concealment. Could he have neutralized both of them, as well?

Draycos let his claws stretch out of their sheaths against Jack's chest in frustration. Even with the enemy's advantage in numbers and positioning, he felt sure he could have defeated all three of them.

Or at least, he could have if he had been on his own. But he wasn't on his own. Jack wasn't trained, either in combat or in evasion. If Draycos had made a move, the boy would most likely have been killed.

Should he have moved before Raven murdered the Wistawki citizens, then? Should he have leaped out and stopped that from happening? Or should he have done something afterward, perhaps, before they put Jack to sleep?

But no. With Raven's arm pressed around Jack's throat Draycos hadn't been able to see properly, but his hearing hadn't been blocked. Never at any time had all three of the enemy been within range for a quick one-one-one attack, and anything else would again have been risking Jack's life.

Risking it for nothing, too, since it seemed clear that they didn't plan to kill him. At least not right away.

Now, of course, it was too late for action of any sort. Jack was fast asleep, drugged by the chemical Raven had injected into his skin. It was one thing to grab the boy in mid-leap and carry him up onto a balcony. It was a different matter entirely to try to run with him balanced across his back.

No. For the moment the enemy had the upper hand. Draycos would have to watch, and wait, and be patient. If they wanted Jack alive, they must also want something from him. That meant they would eventually have to wake him up. Once Jack was again able to move on his own, there would be time to think about escape.

The group reached the spaceport and went inside, making their way around the outer area where the tubes connected.

Draycos eased an eye just far enough up on Jack's chest to see out the V of his shirt. Eventually, he knew, they would reach a ship.

Eventually, they did.

It was a rather impressive ship, if Jack's spacecraft was a proper standard to judge by. It was nearly twice as big as the *Essenay,* with an elaborate sleekness about it that implied wealth and social position. Or at least with the Shontine it would have implied that. He studied the craft as they walked toward it, noting its shape and design and features as best he could. Someday he might need to identify it.

Raven, still in the lead, stopped at the bottom of the gangway and waited for the others to catch up. "All right," he said when they were gathered together. "You know the rendezvous point. We've already lost two weeks with the kid's disappearing act; the boss will skin all of us alive if you don't get him there fast."

"After all this, he'd frinking well better cooperate, too," the one named Drabs grunted.

"Let the boss worry about that part," Raven told him. "You just concentrate on getting him there in one piece, all right?"

"Should we not do a full-body search of him first?" the Brummga asked.

"What for?" Raven scoffed. "Weapons? Escape gear? Pretty tricky to use something like that when you're sound asleep."

"In my profession we do not take unnecessary chances," the Brummga countered stiffly.

"In mine we do what we're told," Raven said, just as stiffly. "You strap him to the bunk, you give him a booster shot every twelve hours, and that's *all* you do. You don't feed him, you don't bathe him, you don't read him bedtime stories. Do I make myself clear?"

"Perfectly," the Brummga rumbled.

"You off, then?" Drabs asked.

Raven nodded. "I'm going to be late as it is. You just get the kid to the boss as fast as you can burn fuel. I'll see you later."

"Right," Drabs said. "Good luck."

Raven nodded and headed back along the tube. Lugging Jack along with them, the others went into the ship.

The trip was much quieter than Draycos had expected it to be. From what he'd gleaned of the Brummga's attitude, he thought the other might disobey the orders about searching Jack. If that had happened, and if he had discovered Draycos, the K'da would have had a difficult decision to make.

But no one searched Jack. In fact, except for the injections Drabs gave him twice each day, no one paid any attention to him at all. It was exactly as if they were couriers delivering a package.

The trip was also quite boring. More than once Draycos thought about going off and exploring the ship, particularly during the hours when everyone seemed to be asleep. But there was no way for him to know what kind of monitoring system might be in place to keep watch on the rooms and corridors. The *Essenay* had such a system—Uncle Virge had made a point of bringing that to his attention early on—and it seemed unlikely that people who engaged in casual murder would neglect such basic security.

He also gave considerable thought to the idea of over-whelming the crew and taking over the ship. Once Drabs's injection schedule was interrupted, Jack would surely regain consciousness. Together, they ought to be able to fly this ship somewhere to freedom.

But again, not knowing exactly what he was up against made that an unacceptably risky move. With only Drabs and the Brummga aboard, he would have had a good chance of defeating them before they realized what was happening. But from the bits of conversation he was able to overhear when Jack's cabin door was open, it was clear that there was a flight crew, as well. Their numbers, their locations, and their routines were all unknown.

Over and over again, his military instructors had told him that a good warrior never took foolish chances unless there was no other alternative. The alternative here was to simply wait.

So he waited. That didn't mean he had to like it.

Finally, after three long days, they arrived.

Back on Vagran, Drabs and the Brummga had carried Jack through the streets like a drunken friend being taken back to his ship. At this end of the trip, they were better prepared with a collapsible stretcher, set up just inside the hatch. The Brummga carried Jack there and laid him on it. Then he and Drabs rolled the boy down the gangway to a waiting ground vehicle.

The back of the vehicle had no windows, but Draycos managed to get a few glances before the doors closed on them. They were in another spaceport, a much bigger one this time. Bouncing along in the darkness inside the vehicle, he wondered if they had reached their final destination or would be trans-ferring to another spacecraft.

The ride was quite short, no more than a few minutes.

There was movement outside the vehicle, and then Drabs opened the rear doors and he and the Brummga rolled Jack's stretcher out onto the ground.

Rising from the ground beside them was the most impressive spacecraft Draycos had seen yet.

He peered out at the vessel as the Brummga rolled the stretcher toward the gangway, a strange sensation stirring inside him. A Shontine ship of this size and design would be either an expensive private yacht or else the business spacecraft of a major corporation. He knew he couldn't jump to that same conclusion in this unfamiliar region of space; but even so, it certainly appeared that someone with great wealth or power or both was interested in Jack. Very interested indeed.

But why? What would anyone want with a young human adrift on his own?

Or was there something about himself that Jack hadn't told him?

It was as he was thinking about that, and studying the ship, that he saw the word-symbols written on the hull beside the entrance.

A fresh surge of emotion flowed into him. Words! Identification words, perhaps. Maybe even the spacecraft's name.

Except that Jack was unconscious and couldn't see them. And Draycos couldn't read human word-symbols.

The K'da stretched his claws in and out of their sheaths in agonized frustration. It was a vital clue, possibly the precise clue Jack needed to learn the truth behind all this. He couldn't afford to let the opportunity slip away.

He would just have to memorize the symbols, that was all. Memorize their shapes and their positioning, so that he could reproduce them later.

But even as he realized what he had to do, he knew with a sinking feeling that the task was beyond his capabilities. There were too many letters there, and his visual memory was simply not good enough to hold their shapes over the hours or days that might elapse before he could show them to Jack.

He would try—he would certainly try. But he knew that he would fail.

Unless . . .

He smiled grimly to himself. No, he couldn't memorize the letters' shapes. But perhaps there was another way. A way that only a poet-warrior of the K'da could use.

Gazing at the symbols as the stretcher was rolled toward the ship, he set to work.

CHAPTER 16

The first thing Jack noticed as he worked his way slowly back toward consciousness was that his neck felt funny.

Not that it hurt. It didn't, really. But it definitely felt funny.

Abruptly, he realized why. He was sitting upright in a chair, with his head bowed down toward his chest. The funny feeling was coming from the back of his neck, strained as it was by the pull of his head.

He was fully awake now. But that didn't mean the rest of the world had to know it. There were soft voices carrying on a quiet conversation somewhere nearby, and there was an equally soft light showing against his eyelids. Maybe if he let them think he was still asleep, he would learn something that would help him get out of here.

Or even figure out exactly where "here" was.

It might also be a good idea to take a quick inventory and see what kind of shape he was in. Aside from his neck, which was starting to feel a little stiff now, nothing hurt. Not even his shins, which should still be tender from Draycos's misfired balcony leap. The fact that they weren't meant he'd been kept asleep for at least a couple of days.

A couple of days of travel time? Probably.

Which, unfortunately, meant he probably wasn't on the Vagran Colony anymore.

So much for getting to the spaceport where the *Essenay* would be waiting. He hoped Uncle Virge had figured that out by now and gotten off the planet.

The lack of pain was the plus side of his physical condition. On the minus side, his stomach felt very empty. Being asleep without eating for a couple of days would do that, too. With his nose six inches from his chest, he also noticed that he was starting to smell a little.

So they'd drugged him with something, tossed him aboard a ship or transport, and lugged him some unknown distance across the Orion Arm. The big question was, where?

The other big question was, why?

"Good afternoon, Jack," a voice said.

It was all Jack could do to keep himself from jerking with reaction. If he lived halfway to forever, that was one voice he knew he would never, ever forget.

It was the cold, heartless, snakelike voice he'd heard on Iota Klestis. The voice of the man in charge of the group sifting through the wreckage of the *Havenseeker*.

Maybe even the man who had ordered the K'da and Shontine ships destroyed in the first place.

"You can lose the act," the voice said, going even colder with impatience. "My instruments tell me you regained consciousness some thirty seconds ago. Don't waste my time."

Slowly, blinking his eyes a couple of times, Jack raised his head.

He was in a small but very nicely furnished room, seated in a chair across from an ornately carved wooden desk. The way the furniture was fastened down, he guessed he was aboard a spaceship.

A group of lights on the desk had been arranged to shine directly into his face. They weren't painfully bright, at least not once his eyes adjusted to them, but they were more than bright enough to wash out his view of whoever or whatever was seated on the other side of the desk.

He also noted that his hands, resting in his lap, were handcuffed together. He'd missed that in his earlier inventory.

"Okay," he said, squinting his eyes a little against the glare of the lights. Fleetingly, he wondered what had happened to Draycos, then put the thought out of his mind. He had enough troubles of his own right now. "I'm awake. What now?"

"I want your uncle," Snake Voice said, his voice coming from behind the lights. "Where is he?"

Jack grimaced. Obvious, of course. They were busy cleaning up loose ends, and Uncle Virge and the *Essenay* were a very sizable loose end. "I don't know," he said.

"I'd advise you not to lie," Snake Voice said, his voice going still colder. "We know perfectly well that he didn't simply desert you on Vagran. You either have a prearranged rendezvous point, or else there are several possible places where you can meet. I want the list."

Jack shook his head. "Look, I really don't know where he is," he said, putting some pleading into his voice.

For a moment Snake Voice sat quietly. Jack forced himself not to squirm, wondering what would be next. A major interrogation, probably, as they tried to find out who else he might have told about the K'da and Shontine.

Then, of course, they would kill him. When he didn't come back, he wondered distantly, would Uncle Virge be smart enough to go to the Internos Police with his story?

Would they believe him even if he did? A ship's computer wasn't exactly a legal witness.

"Well, then, I suppose we'll have to say goodbye," Snake Voice said at last. "If you can't deliver your uncle, then you're of no use to us. We'll just have to kill you and find someone else to help us."

Jack blinked again, nearly missing the threat as his brain latched onto the last part of the sentence. Someone to help them? Was this some sort of lame trick?

And then, with a sudden flash of hope, he realized he'd gotten it all wrong. Snake Voice wasn't here to clean up loose ends on the K'da and Shontine thing, because Snake Voice didn't know Jack was the one who'd stumbled into that mess. This was something else entirely.

And they weren't looking for Uncle Virge, the ship's computer. They were looking for Uncle Virgil, the professional thief and con man.

"Wait a minute," he said. "Are you talking about a job?"

"That's none of your concern," Snake Voice said. "My business is with Virgil Morgan, not some half-grown nephew."

"Oh," Jack said, cocking his head a little to the side. "Gee, that's too bad. Because if you want to talk to Uncle Virgil, you first have to talk to me."

"Watch your mouth, kid," another familiar voice threatened from behind Jack.

He looked back over his shoulder to see Drabs standing guard by the door. "Oh, hello, Drabs," he said, waving his handcuffed hands cheerfully. "Lieutenant Raven step out for a minute?"

Drabs started to sputter something—"So the boy knows

your name," Snake Voice said icily, cutting the other off in mid-sputter. "Both your names. That's very clever, Drabs. Very clever indeed."

Drabs looked about as unhappy as Jack had ever seen a man look. "Sir," he said, his voice pleading. "It's not—I mean, we didn't—it was the Brummga. He—"

"Enough," Snake Voice cut him off again. "I'll speak with you later. Now. Jack."

Jack turned back to face the lights. "Yes?"

"I don't think you realize the seriousness of the situation you're in," Snake Voice said. "Not only did you gun down two innocent Vagran citizens, but you then fled the jurisdiction."

Jack's stomach tied itself into a knot at the memory. "You mean I was kidnapped," Jack corrected him. "And it was Raven who shot them, not me."

"I have three witnesses who will swear in court that you were the one who pulled the trigger," Snake Voice said calmly. "Assuming the case ever reaches a court, that is. Alternatively, the whole unpleasant incident could simply end up in the Va-gran Police 'unsolved' file."

Jack glared past the lights. "The phony theft thing wasn't good enough for you, huh?" he said bitterly. "You had to kill a couple of innocent Wistawki to get me on the hook?"

"In my experience, no one is truly innocent," Snake Voice said offhandedly. "As to the rest, it was you who ruined the previous frame-up."

"Yeah, right," Jack muttered. "Stupid of me. How dare I try to clear myself?"

"And none of it would have been necessary at all if your uncle hadn't made himself so difficult to find," Snake Voice concluded. "If you dislike your current position, take it up with him."

"What, there aren't any other con men in the business anymore?" Jack asked, fishing for information.

There was a short pause, and he had the distinct and uncomfortable feeling that Snake Voice was smiling at him. "Like uncle, like nephew. Virgil Morgan was always squeezing stones, too, trying to pump information out of them."

Jack shrugged. "Can't blame me for trying."

"Oh yes, I could," Snake Voice said. "But I won't. And no, I don't want his con artist skills. What I want is his considerable talent at opening large and well-protected vaults. At that, he's the best there is. And I'm accustomed to having the very best."

"Okay," Jack said. He'd squiggled around long enough, and it was clear now that there was only one way to play this. "What's the job, and what's the pay?"

"As I told you before, that's none of your concern," Snake Voice said.

"And as I told *you* before, if you want Uncle Virgil you have to talk to me," Jack countered. "I mean, there's not much point in being retired if anyone can get hold of you just by picking up a phone."

There was another silence, a long one this time. Jack kept his eyes focused between the desk lights, trying to get a glimpse of whoever was back there. But the best he could do was a vague outline that could have been a man. It could just as easily have been a shaped bonsai tree.

"I must have missed his retirement party," Snake Voice said at last. "Very well. Drabs?"

A few clunking footsteps, and Drabs appeared at Jack's side, glowering down at him. Gripped in his hand was a small metal suitcase. "You sure you want to do this, sir?" he asked. "Personally, I don't trust this kid farther than I can spit him."

"If he crosses us, you can go to Vagran and watch his execution," Snake Voice said. "Open it."

Still glowering, Drabs hoisted the suitcase onto Jack's lap and popped the catches.

There was only a single item in the suitcase, nestled snugly in the center of custom-fitted foam packaging: a slender metal cylinder, eight inches long and three in diameter. A number was stamped into one end: 407662. There were also a handful of connectors and valves jutting out at various places.

"There's a cylinder just like this one in the purser's safe aboard the passenger liner *Star of Wonder*," Snake Voice said. "The job is simply to replace that cylinder with this one."

"Ah," Jack said, trying to sound casual. "Just like that."

"Just like that," Snake Voice assured him. "A simple enough job for a man of Virgil Morgan's talents."

"Naturally," Jack agreed with a sinking feeling in his empty stomach. Right. Breaking into a strongly built and heavily protected vault aboard a luxury starliner should be just a walk in the park.

Maybe for Uncle Virgil it would have been. Problem was, Uncle Virgil was dead. "And what's the pay?"

"He gets his nephew back," Snake Voice said quietly. "In one piece, and with no Vagran warrant for his arrest."

Jack swallowed. "Yeah," he muttered. "Under the circumstances, I think he'll take the job."

"Excellent," Snake Voice said, his voice as calm and untroubled as if he'd just closed some simple business deal. "Drabs, have the bridge set up an InterWorld connection to the office here. Mr. Morgan will be placing a call to his uncle."

"Yes, sir," Drabs said, closing and sealing the suitcase again. Lifting it off Jack's lap, he started back toward the door.

Hesitantly, Jack lifted a finger. "Excuse me, but it's not quite that simple."

"No?" Snake Voice asked, a definite hint of threat in his voice.

"No," Jack said. "I'm not calling Uncle Virgil from here. You put me aboard the *Star of Wonder,* and I'll take it from there."

"Impossible," Snake Voice said. "You're staying here as a guarantee of your uncle's behavior."

Jack lifted his eyebrows. "Then get someone else to do the job."

"You want me to change his mind, sir?" Drabs asked.

"I'd like nothing better," Snake Voice said. "Unfortunately, Morgan will want guarantees that his nephew is unharmed."

"You put him aboard the liner and he'll bolt," Drabs warned. "Sure as anything he will."

"No, I don't think so," Snake Voice said thoughtfully. "He's smart enough to realize that once a warrant is issued on Vagran, he'll never be safe again. Not anywhere in the Orion Arm."

Jack sighed. "Yes, thanks, I've got the message. How far away is the liner?"

"Not far," Snake Voice said. "Across this very spaceport, as a matter of fact. Drabs will take you there and buy you a ticket."

"Fine," Jack said. "What about clothes and tools?"

"You can pick up a change of clothing aboard ship," Snake

Voice said. "As for tools, I presume Morgan will bring his own. When you contact him."

There was a slight shuffling noise, as if the man behind the desk was leaning forward. "You *are* planning to contact him as you promised, aren't you?"

"Don't worry," Jack said, wishing fervently that he *did* have Uncle Virgil to call on. Or even Uncle Virge. "I know how to handle it," he added, trying to sound like he actually did. "I want my stuff back, though."

"Your stuff?"

"My multitool, EvGa, and tangler," Jack told him. "Your people took them from me on Vagran."

"Of course," Snake Voice said. "Drabs will return your multitool before you board the ship. You won't be needing the other items."

"But—"

"Then that's settled," Snake Voice said. "One final point. The liner will leave here early this afternoon, make three more stops, then reach its final destination twelve days from now. Your uncle has just that long to complete his task. I suggest you don't wait too long to contact him."

Twelve days. Terrific. "Sure," Jack said.

"Good. Any questions?"

"Yes, actually," Jack said. "What's in the real cylinder, and who am I stealing it from?"

"So; no questions," Snake Voice said. "Excellent. You'll be contacted again in twelve days. I trust your uncle will be there to give me good news."

An unseen signal passed, and Drabs got a grip on his arm. "On your feet, kid."

Jack did as ordered. Halfway up, a black bag unexpectedly dropped over his head. "Hey!"

"A necessary precaution," Snake Voice said. "Enjoy the cruise."

They were out of the ship and into a land vehicle before the blindfold came off. Even then, they weren't taking any chances: the vehicle was a closed truck, and he and Drabs were in the back. "First class all the way, I see," Jack commented. "Where do I sleep on the liner, the engine room?"

"Funny," Drabs growled. "Don't worry, I'll get you a real nice double cabin. Like the boss said, we want you to enjoy the trip."

They rode the rest of the way in silence. Jack still hadn't had a chance to check on Draycos, but he could feel some slight movement on his skin now. He hoped the dragon was okay.

Finally, they pulled to a stop. "End of the line?" Jack asked.

"For me, yes," Drabs said. "For you, it's the beginning."

"I can hardly wait," Jack muttered, standing up and heading back to the rear doors.

Drabs blocked his way. "I just have one other thing to say to you," he said, his eyes locking onto Jack's face like twin lasers. "The boss told you you'd be in trouble with the cops if you mess this up. What *I'm* telling you is that if you duck out on us, odds are you won't have to worry about the cops. Odds are you'll be dead before they ever catch up with you. Get me?"

"Sure," Jack said tiredly. "Matter of fact, I've had about as much of you as I'd ever want. Can we go now?"

For another minute Drabs continued to glare. Then, he smiled. A very unpleasant smile. "Sure," he said. "Let's go."

CHAPTER 17

Drabs was as good as his word. The cabin he got for Jack was easily the nicest room the boy had ever been in, except for one ground-side hotel suite Uncle Virgil had rented them once during a high-stakes scam.

Of course, the fact that Drabs had kept his promise on the cabin probably meant he would keep other promises, too. Such as his threat to hunt Jack down and kill him if he tried to run.

The first job, after catching up on each other's stories, was to make up for the three days of missed meals. According to the map in his stateroom, the *Star of Wonder* had ten dining rooms and snack bars, four of which were open twenty-four hours a day. The room's status listing showed that Drabs had left a generous credit line for him to draw on, so eating and other incidentals wouldn't be a problem.

But having also lived in the same set of clothes for those same three days, he didn't think the high-paying customers of the liner would appreciate mingling with him over lunch.

Fortunately, his stateroom was fancy enough to have a small food synthesizer set off in one corner. The menu was limited to simple snacks, but there was enough of a selection for him to at least take the edge off his hunger.

Not surprisingly, the synthesizer balked at preparing Draycos's favorite hamburger-and-tuna-and-chocolate-sauce sandwich. Jack solved that problem by ordering a hamburger, a tuna fish sandwich, and a chocolate sundae, then putting them together himself. The dragon had to make do without the motor oil.

After that he took a trip to one of the shops for some changes of clothing, which Draycos insisted on. A shower was next, which Draycos insisted on even more firmly.

With all of what Uncle Virge would have called housekeeping duties out of the way, Jack could finally get down to business. Sprawling across one of the two beds in the shirt and slacks of a suit he'd bought, he began going through the *Star of Wonder*'s information booklets, reading about the ship's services and studying the layouts of the various decks. Draycos, for his part, curled himself up on the chair at the small writing desk across the room, singing softly to himself and doodling on a notepad.

"I don't know, Draycos," Jack sighed, letting the map drop onto the bed and leaning back against the bulkhead. It was hard to believe that after sleeping for three days straight he could be tired, but he was. He was tired, frustrated, and very, very scared. "I feel like I've been dropped into a deep hole, with the whole universe standing on top shoveling dirt in at me. What are we going to do?"

The dragon paused in his singing and looked up. "About what?" he asked, readjusting the stylus he had gripped in one of his front paws.

"What do you mean, about what?" Jack demanded, a flash

of annoyance cutting through the fear. "About this whole stupid situation, that's what. Do you have any idea the kind of security they're going to have on the purser's safe?"

"I do not know," Draycos said. "What is a purser's safe?"

"The purser is the guy on a starliner in charge of money," Jack told him. "His safe is the vault where passengers can store their valuables during the trip."

He waved his hand in a wide sweep around him. "And on a ship like this, there are going to be some really *serious* valuables. Jewelry, data tubes, maybe even some one-of-a-kind art objects. It's going to be like breaking into a bank. Worse than a bank, really, because here there's no place to run after the job."

"You cannot do it?"

Jack shook his head. "Maybe Uncle Virgil could have done it, with the right tools and a week or two to get ready. He was good enough. But I'm not. Not alone."

Draycos's green eyes glittered. "But you are not alone, Jack," he said quietly. "I am here."

Jack gazed at the dragon, a strange feeling stirring inside him. Here was this alien creature, willing to help him out of a tight spot. Not only willing to help, but willing to stick his own neck into danger doing it.

It was like the feeling of slowly starting to thaw out again in a warm room after standing around half frozen in the cold all afternoon. For a moment, despite the trouble he was still in, Jack felt a distant glimmer of hope.

Then the rest of the reality caught up with him. Draycos wasn't doing this out of the goodness of his heart, or whatever was in his chest pumping all that black blood around. He had a fleet full of his people to rescue, and at the moment Jack was the only tool he had. If Jack went down, Draycos went down with him.

The dragon was here, but only until he found someone else to help him carry on his mission. When he did, it would be good-bye.

The warmth faded away, and the cold quietly closed in again. "I appreciate the offer," he said. "But unless you know a really good safecracker within a couple days' flight from here, I don't know how you can help."

"Do not give up hope," Draycos insisted. "I am a poet-warrior of the K'da. I am not without resources."

"Yeah, that must be some course of study," Jack said with a sniff. "Burglary-for-Warriors 102. Must first have taken Burglary-for-Warriors 101."

Draycos flashed his teeth once but made no comment. Bending back over the desk, he resumed his doodling and quiet singing.

Jack frowned at him, starting to feel irritated. His life was hanging by a piece of cobweb, and the dragon was playing with a notepad? "What *are* you doing?" he demanded.

"Attempting to unmask our enemy," Draycos said. "Come and see."

Frowning harder, Jack got up and crossed to the desk.

Draycos hadn't been simply doodling. He had been writing.

Writing?

"The spacecraft you were brought aboard had these words beside the entrance," Draycos explained, touching the notepad with the tip of his tongue. "Because the human Drabs took care to cover your eyes when you left, we may assume the words are important."

"Probably the name of the ship," Jack said, his heart starting to beat faster. "But I thought you said you didn't read or write our language."

"I do not," Draycos said.

"You memorized the shapes, then?"

"Not directly," the dragon said. "Alien symbols are difficult for one unfamiliar with them to memorize. But I am a poet-warrior of the K'da; and so as you were taken aboard the ship, I composed a song."

Jack blinked. "A *song?*"

"Yes. Observe."

Draycos set the stylus against the paper. "And to the right, from tail to head," he sang, "stands single soldier, tall but dead."

He drew a slightly wavy line that did indeed look kind of like a K'da seen from above. A capital "I," Jack decided, drawn in a stylized form.

"Just like the first; again it stands," Draycos went on. "Two soldiers lean to, with joined hands."

He drew two more wavy lines, this time at an inverted-V angle that connected at the top. Another wavy line connected them midway up. An "A"?

"A Shontine waits to hear a sound; shall two eyes listen at the ground?"

He drew a vertical line, with two gogglelike eyes beside it. Seen from the side, Jack had to admit, it *did* look like the two eyes of someone with his ear pressed against the ground.

Seen upright, of course, it was a capital "B."

"Squeezed ring of fire; and what is more," Draycos sang, "a fire burns within its core."

A capital "O" with some sort of marking in the center. Jack couldn't tell what the mark was supposed to be, but it didn't matter. The thing was definitely an "O."

"A blade thrusts left, to base of hedge; naught can be seen except the edge."

Jack smiled at that one. It was a capital "L," with the same waviness as the other letters. Now that he thought about it, it did indeed look like light shining off the edge of a knife point with the rest of the knife in shadow. Draycos had an interesting way of looking at things.

"Stands final soldier, single one." Draycos drew another "I." "Hand down, for now the tale is done."

He laid down the stylus. "And it is finished," he added.

"I will be dipped in butter," Jack said, shaking his head in admiration. "That was just plain flat-out brilliant."

"I merely made use of my talents and training," Draycos said modestly. Still, to Jack's ear he sounded pleased at the praise. "As you do yourself. Tell me, what do the words say?"

Jack swiveled the paper around to face him. *"Advocatus Diaboli,"* he read. "Huh."

"You recognize the name?" Draycos asked.

Jack scratched his cheek. "I don't even recognize the words," he said, swiveling the desk computer around and punching for a dictionary. After all of that work, and his own compliments, he hoped Draycos hadn't messed up with this somewhere. "It doesn't even sound like English."

He typed in the words. "Aha," he said, nodding as the page came up. "It didn't sound like English because it isn't. It's a phrase in Old Latin: 'Devil's Advocate.' Says that's someone who argues against an authority's point of view. Odd name for a ship. Was there anything else written there?"

"There were no other words," Draycos said. "But beneath

them was a small design. It may have been the same as the one on the sealed warehouse door."

Jack felt his throat tighten. "You mean the Braxton Universis logo?"

"It may have been," Draycos said. "As I have said, it is difficult to memorize alien designs."

"No, you nailed it just fine," Jack said sourly. "A Braxton cargo, a Braxton ship. The whole thing was Braxton, right from the start."

"But for what purpose?"

"How should I know?" Jack snapped, swiveling the computer back around. "A fancy plot to take down some rival, maybe. A big corporate merger that someone won't play ball over. How in blazes should I know?"

He stomped across the room and flopped back onto the bed, glaring bleakly into a corner of the room. All along, he'd been clinging to the hope that the Braxton cargo part had been pure coincidence. That it was some old rival of his uncle's looking for vengeance, not something coming at him from Braxton Universis itself.

But thanks to Draycos's cleverness, that hope was now shattered. This was some corporate game, all right. The vast power of Braxton Universis was on one side, some unknown player was on the other, and Jack Morgan was dead-center in the middle of it.

"You are troubled."

Jack shifted his glare to Draycos. "Your bet your tail I'm troubled," he growled. "And if you had any brains, you would be, too. This is *Cornelius Braxton* we're up against."

He took another look at the dragon's face, and instantly

regretted his words. "I'm sorry," he said, a layer of guilt adding to the rest of his misery. "I know you just don't know."

"I am not offended," Draycos assured him. "Tell me about him."

"What's to tell?" Jack asked, shrugging uncomfortably. "In a spiral arm's worth of hardball businessmen, Braxton's one of the hardest. He inherited a business from his father and built it into an empire. He's smart, he's ruthless, and he gets whatever he wants."

Pulling the metal suitcase from under his bed, he opened it. "And whatever he's up to this time, this thing is the key," he said, taking out the cylinder. "I wish I knew what was in it."

"Or what is in the one you are to switch it for," Draycos said.

"That, too," Jack agreed glumly, peering at the cylinder. "I don't know whether he's trying to plant this one on someone, or get the other one away from him. Either way, when the roof caves in, there's only going to be one fall guy."

"Pardon?"

"Fall guy," Jack repeated. "The guy who takes the fall, the blame for something someone else did. In this case, me."

Draycos uncoiled from the chair and padded over to Jack's side. "What then do you propose we do?"

For a moment Jack had the sudden urge to stroke the dragon's head, just like he might have petted a dog. He resisted the impulse. "I don't know," he confessed, turning the cylinder over in his hand instead. "Remember, I'm their guarantee of Uncle Virgil's good behavior. If they were willing to let me out of their sight, it's because I'm not going to *be* out of their sight."

Draycos twitched the tip of his tail. "They will have someone watching you."

"Watching me, and watching for Uncle Virgil," Jack said. "That means I can't run and I can't call the police. *And* I can't just sit around and do nothing. What's left?"

The dragon was silent a moment. "There is a style of warfare the K'da call *koi shike,*" he said. "It speaks of a large stone thrown into quiet water to force a response from hiding fish."

"Yeah, we've got something like that, too," Jack growled. "We call it 'rocking the boat.' What's your point?"

Draycos ran a paw thoughtfully along the side of the cylinder. "Let us do as they demand," he said. "Let us steal the item and replace it with this duplicate. We will then follow the ripples from the stone and see where they lead."

Jack snorted. "You make it sound so easy."

"I am a warrior of the K'da," Draycos said. "You are skilled in the arts of theft and cunning. Together we can surely find a way."

Jack shook his head. "I wouldn't bet on that," he warned. "But I don't have anything better to offer."

He returned the cylinder to its hiding place under the bed and stood up. "I guess the least we can do is go take a look at the safe," he added, stepping to the closet and getting out the suit coat that went with his new shirt and slacks. "You coming?"

Draycos's response was to leap in through Jack's opennecked shirt. "And then?" the dragon asked from his shoulder.

Jack took a deep breath. "We'll come up with something. I hope."

CHAPTER 18

The purser's office was bigger than Jack had expected, probably four times as big as his own stateroom. It had a chest-high counter extending across the entire room near the door, where the purser stood dealing with passengers who wanted to store their valuables. Behind the counter, another man and woman dressed in white uniforms worked at computer desks, presumably keeping track of what was in the safe and doing other odd jobs.

The safe was bigger than Jack had expected, too. It was more like a small bank vault, easily big enough for three or four people to walk inside. Probably big enough for them to dance in, too. There was a flat metal plate over the spot where the keypad or combination dial would be on a normal safe door. There were also two emergency lights set into the upper walls, one pointed at the vault, the other pointed at the door.

All this he got from a single pass by the open door. The outer door itself, he noted, had a standard lock setup. "We are not going in?" Draycos asked as Jack continued down the corridor.

"In a minute," Jack said. A hundred feet down the corridor

from the purser's office was one of the ship's bars, with a small lounge area across the hallway from it. On the far side of the lounge was a glass wall that looked down onto a casino one deck below. "I thought we might like to come up with a plan first," he added, stepping into the lounge.

"Would not our room be safer?" Draycos murmured as Jack selected a table by the glass wall, well away from the other half dozen people who were talking or sipping drinks.

"This is safe enough," Jack assured him, swiveling his chair around so that he could look down into the casino. With his back to the rest of the lounge, no one would see his lips moving as he and Draycos talked.

At the same time, the faint reflections in the glass would let him keep an eye on the people coming and going in the lounge and corridor behind him. If Snake Voice's agent aboard the *Star of Wonder* got careless, Jack might be able to spot him.

It took somewhat longer than the minute Jack had suggested. It took nearly an hour, in fact, plus three fizzy-sodas, for them to hammer out a workable plan.

At least, Jack hoped it was workable.

The purser was talking with an elderly woman when Jack returned to the office. He waited behind her as patiently as he could, casually looking around for anything he might have missed on his earlier stroll past the place. It was pretty much as he'd noted then, except that above the door were two more emergency lights. Taking several deep breaths, as Uncle Virgil had taught him to do, he tried to relax.

Finally, the woman left. "May I help you, young man?" the purser asked with a smile as Jack stepped up to the counter.

"Yes, sir, I hope so," Jack said, pitching his tone and manner to make himself seem a couple of years younger than he really was. Uncle Virgil had always said that the younger you were, the less likely people were to suspect you of being trouble. "I'm Jack Morgan, Stateroom 332. My uncle wanted me to put one of his data tubes in the safe."

"Certainly," the purser said. "Do you have a deposit box?"

"No, not yet," Jack said. "How long will it take to get one?"

"No time at all," the purser assured him, stepping to one side and lifting a section of the countertop. His other hand, Jack noted, stayed out of sight beneath the edge of the counter as he did so. There must be either a release catch he needed to operate or an alarm he had to deactivate. The purser propped up the section of countertop and pulled open the swinging door beneath it. "If you'll come this way, please?"

He led the way back to the vault and swung the metal plate back to reveal a keypad set into the door. "If you'll just stand there, sir?" he said, indicating a spot where the plate would block Jack's view of the keypad.

Jack did as he was told, and the purser began punching in the code. The plate covering the keypad had seemed easy enough to move, with no secret switches the purser had to use first. But Jack had already noticed the heavy ring the purser was wearing on that hand. Probably a short-range radio transmitter that identified him and deactivated the plate's alarms.

It was like a bank, all right, with all the cute security tricks anyone could ever want. A terrible place to have to break into.

It was just as well, Jack thought, that he wasn't going to have to do that.

"There we go," the purser announced, swinging the plate back over the keypad. He pulled on the handle, and the heavy door swung ponderously open.

Jack had been wrong about one thing: there was not, in fact, enough room in there for anyone to dance. Both walls were lined with locked deposit boxes of various sizes, with only a narrow walkway down the middle. "Let me see, now," the purser said, studying a pocket computer he'd pulled from a belt pouch. "Box 48 is free. That one will have plenty of room for your data tube. Unless you think your uncle may want to add other items later in the voyage?"

"Oh," Jack said, frowning. "I hadn't thought of that."

He stepped into the vault, as if trying to get a closer look at the boxes. They were, he noted with a small bit of relief, standard coded-key types that he should be able to open with his multitool. That part, at least, should be easy.

"Because I know he has some other nice things," he went on, pressing his back tightly against one side of the vault as he pretended to study the boxes on the other side. On his skin, he could feel Draycos shift position as the dragon curled himself over the deposit box doors and peered inside. "How big are these other boxes?"

"They're different sizes," the purser said. "The ones like 48 are three by three by twenty . . ."

He began to rattle off his list of box sizes. Jack pretended to listen, moving slowly down the line of boxes. Draycos was still shifting position, but so far he hadn't given the signal.

The purser had finished his list by the time Jack made it to the far end of the vault. "And how much are the different rental fees?" he asked, waiting for Draycos to come out of his curve and get all the way onto his back again.

He felt the dragon do so. Turning around, he pressed his back against the other side of the vault.

"There's no cost for any of them," the purser said, a note

of puzzlement creeping into his voice. He was probably used to people wanting to step into his vault. He probably *wasn't* used to people wanting to make a vacation home out of the place.

Which meant that Jack had better wrap this up quick, before the man's surprise turned into suspicion.

"Because there's that necklace he got for Aunt Louise," Jack said, as if talking to himself. "And the antique humidor— that's pretty big. I don't know if he's going to want to keep that in the cabin or not."

Draycos stirred one final time, and the tip of a claw delicately touched Jack's ribs.

The dragon had found the cylinder.

"No," Jack said as if suddenly making up his mind. "No, number 48 should do just fine."

He turned around, stepping away from the boxes, and idly ran a fingertip down the boxes he'd been leaning against. "I guess he can always come and change to one of these bigger boxes if he needs to, right?"

"Certainly," the purser said. "If you'll step out here, I'll code a key for you."

Jack's finger touched Box 125; and as it did so, Draycos touched a claw to his side again.

Bingo.

"Sure," Jack said, walking out of the vault. The purser went in and slid a key into the lock of Box 48. He connected the key to a thin wire leading to his pocket computer and started tapping buttons.

As he did so, Jack looked casually over at the inside of the vault door. It was there, right where he'd seen it on nearly all the walk-in vaults he'd watched Uncle Virgil crack. Most

Orion Arm safety regulators considered it prudent, most safe-crackers considered it stupid, and most vault owners never considered it at all.

A small red lever labeled *Emergency Door Release,* and a set of glow-in-the-dark instructions on how to use it.

The purser finished his coding and stepped out of the vault. "Here you go," he said, pulling the wire off the key and handing it to Jack. "You can go ahead and put in your data tube now."

"Thank you." Jack took the key and went back into the vault. The key hummed in the lock of Box 48 and popped it open, and he put the data tube inside. He closed it, the key hummed again, and the box was locked. "When do you close tonight?" he asked as he left the vault.

"We're open until midnight," the purser told him, pushing the vault door shut. "We reopen at six in the morning."

"I'll tell my uncle that," Jack said, crossing to the counter and waiting for the purser to open up that section for him again. The purser did so; and from this side, Jack could see that there *was* a button down there that he had to push first. "Thank you."

"Good evening, young man."

Jack left the office and headed back in the direction of the lounge. "You found the cylinder?" he asked, just to make sure.

"Yes," Draycos said. "There were also several data tubes and a small box of jewelry inside."

"Jewelry, huh?" Jack commented. Just ahead on the left was a door marked *Authorized Personnel Only.* "I wonder if the cylinder belongs to a woman."

"Could a woman be a likely target for Braxton Universis?" Draycos asked.

"Oh, sure," Jack said, glancing both ways down the corridor as he reached the door. No one was looking. He tapped the plate, the door slid open, and he ducked through.

Behind the door was a narrow service hallway. Four or five doors led off it to the right, while the end was blocked by a heavy-looking door with a keypad.

Unlike the door he'd entered through, that one would be locked. Fortunately, he didn't need to go that far. What he was looking for should be right here in the corridor.

"Women control lots of corporations," he went on, starting slowly down the hallway. As he walked he ran his fingers along the molded plastic wall on his left, the wall of the purser's office. "Or I suppose the jewelry could be just a gift."

"What do you search for?" Draycos asked, the top of his head rising slightly out of Jack's shoulder.

"Keep down, will you?" Jack growled. "Did you happen to notice the emergency lights back in the purser's office? Small boxes on the walls near the ceiling with lights sticking out of them?"

"I did."

"The boxes contain the lights' batteries," Jack explained. "Here, they almost certainly also contain hidden security cameras. We'll need to knock them out."

His fingers paused, feeling the slight unevenness beneath the plastic wall that meant he'd found a vertical support. "This should be it," he said, turning around and pressing his back to the wall. "There should be a junction box somewhere near here—a small square thing with five wires coming out one side and two out the other. See if you can find it."

Obediently, Draycos shifted around again on his skin. "Well?" Jack asked.

There was no answer. Jack moved slowly along the wall, feeling his heart starting to pound again. Any minute now one of the ship's crew could stumble across him here. The last thing he wanted was to have to come up with a story about why he was leaning against a wall in a place he wasn't supposed to be.

"I believe I have found it," Draycos spoke up in that strange near-far voice that seemed to go with this particular K'da trick. "Are the wires black with silver striping?"

"That's them," Jack confirmed. "Okay, get back aboard; I'm going to turn around."

The dragon drew back from the wall and returned to his back. Jack turned around and held out a hand to the wall. "Show me where it was."

Some weight came onto his forearm. His jacket sleeve puffed out slightly as Draycos's foreleg appeared, sliding out the cuff along Jack's wrist. One of the claws extended and scratched a small curved mark into the wall.

"Great," Jack said as the weight of the dragon's leg melted back onto his skin. Fortunately, this jacket material was more flexible than the leather of his normal coat. "Next stop is the monitor room."

"What is that?"

"The place where people watch the view from the security cameras," Jack explained as he sneaked out of the service corridor and back into the passenger areas. "Especially those in the purser's office."

"You have not spoken of this part of your plan," Draycos said, sounding suspicious.

"Don't worry, we're not going looking for a fight," Jack assured him. "I'm a thief, not a one-man army."

"You are a former thief," Draycos corrected. "And there are two of us."

"Yeah. Whatever."

Not surprisingly, the monitor room hadn't been marked on the floor plans in Jack's stateroom. However, the main security office *had* been shown, and it seemed reasonable that the people staring at the monitor screens would be someplace nearby.

They were, hidden behind another locked door at the end of another dead-end service hallway. "Okay," Jack muttered, moving down the service hallway as quietly as he could. Too late, now, he wondered if this hallway had its own security camera. If it did, he could expect company any minute now.

But no one appeared, and no voice demanded to know what he was doing there. Chewing at his lip, he kept going.

Aside from the door at the far end, this hallway had only two other doors leading off of it. They were situated opposite each other near the far end. As he got closer, he could see that the door on the left had a number and the word *Electrical* on it, while the one on the right said *Storage*.

"Okay," he muttered to Draycos. " 'Storage' here will probably be security stuff. It'll be seriously locked, and we'll be in real trouble if we get caught messing with it."

He turned to the other door. "So let's try in here."

That door was locked, too, but not seriously. A minute with his multitool and Jack had it open. Checking both ways down the hallway, he slipped inside, closing the door behind him.

It was a typical electrical closet, like a hundred others he'd seen in a lifetime of lurking in shadows. Most of the space was taken up by a large electrical switchboard, with wires connecting to a hundred different in-plugs and out-plugs. Other wires were laid out neatly along the walls, going off to other rooms in the area.

But Jack didn't really care about any of that. What he *did* care about were the two large air vents set into the wall, one near the ceiling, the other near the floor.

It was another minute's work with the multitool to take the grating off the lower vent. Twisting his neck awkwardly in the cramped space, he eased his head into the opening. With cool air flowing down the back of his neck he found himself gazing at a similar grill a few feet away. It was the air system grill in the monitor room, and the air flow was going in that direction.

Perfect.

"Okay," he muttered, easing his head back out and fastening the grating back in place. "That's it."

He opened the door and cautiously looked outside. The hallway was still empty. A dozen nervous steps later, and he was safely back in the passenger area of the liner.

"We will obtain the cylinder now?" Draycos asked as Jack strode along.

Jack shook his head. "First we go back to the room," he said. "I've got a couple more things I have to do."

"And then?"

Jack took a deep breath. "Then I guess the job is on."

CHAPTER 19

Jack stopped at one of the dining rooms first, following Uncle Virgil's standard rule that you never went into a job on an empty stomach. He made sure to order far more than he wanted, and brought the leftovers back to the stateroom where Draycos would have the privacy he needed.

As the dragon attacked the rest of the medium-rare T-bone steak, Jack sat at the writing desk putting together a small but very smelly smoke bomb.

It didn't take long. One of his duties for Uncle Virgil had been to create diversions, both for the jobs themselves and also sometimes for when things went suddenly sour and they had to run for their lives. Uncle Virgil had taught him a lot about such things, and Jack had picked up other bits and pieces from some of Uncle Virgil's friends. Even on a luxury starliner, he'd had no trouble buying or scrounging everything he'd needed.

The rest of the preparations didn't take very long, either. Soon—much too soon—everything was ready.

After that, there was nothing to do but wait.

"You are troubled," Draycos said.

Jack looked up from the solitaire game he had laid out on

the writing desk. Draycos had finished his meal and was lying on his stomach beside the bed, his head laid along his front paws in that doglike resting pose of his. All the dragon needed, Jack thought, was a roaring fireplace behind him to complete the picture. "What?"

"I said you are troubled," Draycos repeated, raising his head to look more closely at Jack. "Are you concerned about the mission?"

"Maybe a little," Jack said, looking down at his game. He didn't remember this card layout at all. Apparently, he'd been playing on pure autopilot. "No, I think it'll go all right. The people who designed the system couldn't possibly have expected the approach we're going to use. No, it should work."

"Than what is your concern?"

Slowly, Jack began collecting the cards. "I've been thinking," he said. "I'm wondering if maybe we should forget this whole toss-the-rock-in-the-water thing of yours."

"The *koi shike*?"

"Yeah, that," Jack said. "Maybe we should just switch the cylinders like they told us to and leave it at that."

Draycos's green eyes were glittering. "Do you suggest we allow them to succeed?"

"Look, Draycos, they're going to succeed no matter what we do," Jack said. "I mean, this is *Cornelius Braxton* we're talking about. If he wants this cylinder, or if he wants the cylinder's owner out of his way, then sooner or later he's going to do it. *And* he'll roll over anyone who gets in front of him."

He looked away from Draycos's gaze. "Why should that be us?"

For a moment the dragon was silent. Jack shuffled the cards, not daring to look up at him. Once before, he'd wondered what K'da warriors did to someone who disobeyed orders. Now, he found himself wondering what they did to deserters.

"Uncle Virge does not think you should follow the K'da warrior ethic," Draycos said at last.

Jack looked up sharply. "What makes you say that?"

"You and he discussed it," Draycos said. "In the Vagran spaceport."

Jack made a face. He'd forgotten how good the dragon's ears were. "That was a private conversation, you know."

"My apologies," Draycos said. He didn't sound all that apologetic. "The fact remains that Uncle Virge sees all actions and plans of action in terms of whether they will aid you or harm you."

"What's wrong with that?" Jack demanded. "Who else is going to think about what I need?"

"I agree that you should take care of yourself," Draycos said. "But there should also be more to guide your decisions and actions than simply your own comfort or safety."

"Let me guess," Jack growled. "Doing for others. The noble cause of good versus evil. Sacrificing yourself for a higher purpose. Am I getting warm?"

"You speak with scorn," Draycos said calmly. "But you are correct. There are times when each person must choose his path based solely on what he knows to be right."

Jack sniffed. "The K'da warrior ethic."

"It has nothing to do with warriors," Draycos said. "Nor does it depend on whether you are alone or surrounded by friends and allies. It is a decision of the will, guided by the inner knowledge of right and wrong."

He cocked his head. "Do you still know right and wrong, Jack Morgan?"

"If we go up against Cornelius Braxton, I'll probably die," Jack said bluntly. "Even if I live, I'll go to prison on Vagran for two murders I didn't commit. Is that what you want?"

"If you do not stand against him, the two Wistawki will still be dead," Draycos reminded him. "And you will have to live with the knowledge that their murderer was not brought to justice. Is that what *you* want?"

"I could live with it," Jack said stubbornly.

The green eyes continued to bore into him. Jack tried to hold that gaze, but after a few seconds he gave up. "No, not really," he conceded.

"And you will also know that through their deaths another person was harmed," Draycos went on. "The owner of the cylinder you intend to steal."

"So what do you want me to do?" Jack asked. "Throw *my* life away, too? Add one more death to this whole ugly list?"

"I do not suggest you deliberately sacrifice your life without care," Draycos said. "That is not the way of a warrior. We will be subtle and quiet, and use all the skill and cunning we possess. But the cylinder must be returned to its rightful owner, and that owner warned of the attack against him or her."

Jack shook his head. "I already told you, Draycos. We can't fight Cornelius Braxton and win."

"Then do not fight him because you expect to win," Draycos said. "Fight him because it is the right thing to do."

Jack snorted. "Like pulling that guy Dumbarton out of the hot dirt on Iota Klestis?"

"Yes," Draycos said. "I do not expect any gain from that action. Nor do I expect Dumbarton to be grateful if our lives should cross again. I did it because it was right."

Jack looked down at the cards in his hand. Uncle Virge

would argue strongly against this, he knew. He would remind Jack that there was no one to look after Jack Morgan but Jack Morgan himself. He would point out that high-level corporate warfare was none of Jack's business, and that the sooner he got himself out of the middle of it the better.

But Uncle Virge wasn't here.

"Easy for you to say," he muttered. "I'm the one on the hot seat. You've got nothing to lose."

"On the contrary," Draycos said. "I have the lives of all my people."

Jack looked up, startled. "What?"

"The man behind the desk in the *Advocatus Diaboli*," Draycos said. "You perhaps did not recognize his voice. It was the same human who led those searching the *Havenseeker*."

Jack felt his stomach churn. "Yeah, I recognized it, too," he admitted. "I guess . . . I hoped I was wrong."

"It was the same human," Draycos said firmly. "Thus I face the same decision you do. Do I obey his orders, and sacrifice the owner of the cylinder, and be free afterward to seek him out? Or do I take my stand here against him, and thus risk the lives of all the K'da and Shontine?"

Jack sighed. "You're not thinking this through," he said. "Bad enough when it was just your Valahgua and some pirates or mercenaries they picked up along the way. But with Braxton Universis in the game . . ."

He shook his head. "We can't fight the whole Orion Arm, Draycos," he said quietly. "I don't know what Braxton has against your people, or how he got involved with this. But we can't fight him *and* whoever else he's got in his pocket *and* this Death weapon."

For a moment the dragon was silent. "If what you say is

true, the odds against us are indeed immense," he said at last. "But again, odds do not alter the rightness or wrongness of a course of action. And I believe we have already determined what that right course of action should be."

Jack smiled wanly. "So in other words, you want to take on Braxton Universis," he said. "Just you and me."

"We must of course begin with just you and me," Draycos agreed. "But that does not mean we will not gather allies to our side as we go. The owner of the cylinder, for one, may be grateful for our assistance."

Jack shook his head again. "I can just hear what Uncle Virge would have to say about this."

"I can imagine that, as well," Draycos said. "But the question is what *you* have to say."

Jack sighed. "The Orion Arm's a big place," he said. "Even Cornelius Braxton must have better things to do than track down some punk-nosed kid who messed up on him. Sure, let's give it a shot."

Draycos ducked his head. "I am proud of you, Jack," he said. "Though you are only a boy, you have the spirit of a K'da warrior."

"Yeah, well, let's hope that spirit doesn't get permanently separated from the rest of me tonight," Jack said sourly, looking at his watch. "It's after eleven. I guess we'd better start getting ready."

The *Essenay,* he knew, would be waiting at the rendezvous point on Aldershot by now. Dimly, he wondered what Uncle Virge would do when he simply vanished.

CHAPTER 20

The purser's office was set to close at midnight. Jack got there at exactly five minutes till.

The purser and his two assistants were in the process of closing up for the night as Jack stepped in through the door. "Oh, wait a minute," he called, putting a little pleading into his voice. "Please? Am I too late to put something else in the safe?"

"Not at all, young sir," the purser assured him, coming over to the counter. "Your uncle remembered something else?"

"Yeah." Jack shook his head. "He is so absentminded sometimes."

"No problem," the purser said. "Come on back."

He opened the counter section and walked Jack to the back. Again making sure Jack couldn't see the keypad, he opened the vault. "You have your key?"

"Right here," Jack said, pulling out the key and an expensive-looking jewelry case. Like the data tube he'd put in earlier, he'd bought the jewelry case at one of the liner's gift shops. But of course the purser wouldn't know that. "I really appreciate this."

"Not a problem," the purser said, finishing the combination and pulling open the safe door.

Jack stepped inside and opened Box 48. Laying the jewelry case carefully inside, he closed and locked the box again. "That it?" the purser asked as Jack stepped out of the vault.

"Yes, thank you," Jack said, pausing right by the edge of the door.

Now came the tricky part. Cupping his right hand around the cuff link he was palming, he threw a quick look at each of the purser's assistants. Busy with their computers, neither was looking his direction.

"Watch yourself," the purser warned. Leaning his weight against the door, he started to push it closed.

"I'm okay," Jack said, glancing sideways at the hidden security cameras over the office door. They could be more of a problem, but it didn't look like either of them would have a clear view, either.

The door swung almost closed; and with a sudden twitch of his right wrist, Jack sent the cufflink he was holding clattering onto the floor toward the counter. "Blast!" he said.

It was probably the oldest distraction in the universe. But as Uncle Virgil had been fond of pointing out, the old tricks got old precisely because they worked. Even as he continued pushing the vault door closed, the purser's eyes automatically went to the cuff link bouncing across his floor.

And as Jack threw up his hands in a gesture of frustration, his left hand dipped for a split-second behind the nearly closed door.

Draycos was ready. With a brief tug of weight, he shot out of Jack's sleeve through the gap and into the safe.

Jack's arms continued their upward swing, his left hand moving clear of the vault door just as it slammed shut with a muffled thud. "Darn it all, anyway," Jack growled, chasing after the cuff link. "I am forever losing that thing."

"Let me see it," the purser offered as Jack caught up with the cuff link and picked it up. "Maybe it can be fixed."

"I don't know how anyone could," Jack said, handing it over. He didn't know if the man was suspicious or just trying to be helpful, but it didn't matter. Uncle Virgil had long ago taught him to watch the details, and he'd made sure to carefully break the cuff link. "See how this connector piece flops around?"

"Yes, I see," the purser agreed, twisting it back and forth. "We do have a licensed jeweler aboard, in Gantor Gems down on Deck 17. She may be able to fix it for you."

"That's a good idea," Jack said as the man handed back the cuff link. "Maybe I'll go see her tomorrow. Thanks."

"You're welcome," the purser said, ushering him through the counter opening and out the door. "Have a good night."

Well, a busy night, anyway, Jack told himself as he left the office and headed back down the corridor. First stop would be back to their stateroom for a change of clothing, including the thin plastic gloves he always carried in a hidden pocket in his jacket, and to pick up the rest of the props for the night's performance. He just hoped Draycos would remember the instructions he'd given him for working that emergency release lever.

He also hoped the dragon wasn't claustrophobic.

He had to walk past the monitor room a half dozen times before the area was clear enough for him to sneak into the service hallway without being seen. He got the electrical room door open, slipped inside, and started work on the air vent grill.

He had it halfway off when there was a sudden commotion outside his door. He froze, crouched by the vent, sure that he'd been spotted and that the jig was up.

But the voices and footsteps went past without anyone pounding on his door or trying to open it. The noise faded away, and he realized to his limp relief that it had been nothing but the one o'clock shift change. Wiping the sweat off his forehead, he got back to work.

A minute later the grill was off. Pulling his homemade smoke bomb from a side pocket, he set it carefully into the air conduit and started the fuse. In exactly twenty minutes, if he'd done the job right, the bomb would go off. When it did, the air flow would blow the smoke straight into the monitor room.

It took him seventeen of those twenty minutes to get back to the corridor outside the purser's office. Again, it took him a few tries before he could get into the service hallway without being seen.

Exactly nineteen minutes after setting the bomb, he was in position.

For that last minute he stood in the hallway, counting down the seconds in his mind and staring at the curved mark Draycos had made on the wall. For him, the waiting had always been the hardest part of any job. That was when all the doubts came swirling in: doubts about whether he'd covered all the details, whether someone was off their usual schedule, whether there was some vital bit of information he didn't know or had forgotten.

Sometimes, there had been doubts of a more serious sort.

Questions about whether he should even be doing this sort of work.

Uncle Virgil had done his best to make sure that last set of doubts didn't raise their heads very often. When they did, he'd done his best to brush them aside. That was probably why it hadn't been until after his death that Jack had been able to even start thinking about quitting the business.

Yet here he was, at it again. Only this time it was a K'da warrior who was doing his best to convince him he was doing the right thing.

One of these days, Jack promised himself, he would have to start thinking these things out for himself.

Twenty minutes. Jack listened hard, but even a loud fire alarm from the monitor room would be impossible to hear this far away. Still, if commercial fire procedures hadn't changed in the past couple of years, everyone should be scrambling out of the monitor room right now as the place filled with smoke. The firefighters would then go in, extinguishers at the ready, hunting for the source of the fire.

It wouldn't take them long to find the smoke bomb. Even if they didn't, the bomb would quickly run out of smoke on its own.

But for those crucial few minutes, no one should be watching the camera monitors. Which meant no one would notice if a few of those cameras suddenly blanked out.

Of course, commercial fire procedures *could* have changed in the past couple of years. If they had, he would find that out very soon.

He gave the people in the monitor room another minute to clear out completely. Then, pulling out a steak knife he'd borrowed from the dining room, he set the point against the mark Draycos had made on the wall. Hoping fervently that the dragon had made it *exactly* over the junction box, he shoved the blade into the wall with all his strength.

There was no flash of fire or crackle of electrical sparks. Nothing at all, in fact, to tell him whether or not the cameras had been knocked out of action.

If they hadn't been shut down, he would find that out very soon, too.

Twenty seconds' work with his multitool and he had the door to the purser's office open. Slipping inside, he closed the door behind him and turned on the lights.

No one was waiting for him inside. Jumping onto and over the counter, he went straight to the vault. With the end of his multitool, he pounded on the door with the thud-thud, thud-thud signal they'd agreed on.

For a dozen seconds nothing happened. A dozen horrible thoughts ran through Jack's mind in that time. Had Draycos not heard him? Had he panicked in the enclosed space? Was he lying whimpering in a corner, unable to move? Had the release lever malfunctioned, trapping him inside? Had he already suffocated?

There was a click from the lock, and to his relief the door started to slowly swing outward.

He grabbed the handle and pulled. The thing was heavier than he'd realized. But they got it open, and Draycos bounded out. "The exit mechanism is indeed as you said," he commented. The dragon was as calm as if he'd just been for a walk in the park, instead of being locked in a large metal coffin for over an hour. "A useful yet puzzling design."

"It's a safety feature, in case someone gets accidentally locked inside," Jack said, brushing past him into the vault. Setting himself in front of Box 125, he set hurriedly to work. "Like Uncle Virgil once told me, all the best tricks are already done before the magician snaps his fingers."

"You seem hurried," Draycos said. "Is there trouble?"

"There's always trouble," Jack told him. "In this case, even if I knocked out the cameras, there's probably a signal that goes off when the vault door is opened."

"Why did you not disarm it?"

"I couldn't," Jack told him. "It would be a separate self-contained system. But if I'm fast enough—ah."

The box popped open. "Get ready to help me close the vault door," Jack told Draycos, pulling out the cylinder and replacing it with the one from his inner coat pocket. Putting the real cylinder into his pocket, he closed the box and locked it. "Okay, let's go," he said, stepping out of the vault.

Together, they shoved the door closed. Half a minute later they were outside the purser's office, Draycos riding Jack's back, heading down the corridor toward the lounge where they'd done their planning that afternoon. "Should you not have locked the outer door?" Draycos asked from his headrest on Jack's right shoulder.

"No point," Jack told him as he stripped off his plastic gloves and tucked them away in a side pocket. Was that the sound of running footsteps he could hear coming down the corridor behind him? No, it was just his imagination. "They already know someone's been in there. Come on, this sort of work always makes me thirsty."

He was sitting in the bar ordering a fizzy-soda when the first group of security men went pounding past.

CHAPTER 21

He gave the situation back at the purser's office forty minutes and two fizzy-sodas to come to a nice boil. Then, leaving the bar, he strolled back that direction.

Bad news, Uncle Virgil had often told him, was the only thing in the universe that traveled faster than the speed of light. Jack had never quite believed it; but as he approached the office he had to admit that maybe Uncle Virgil had had a point.

There were probably twenty people crowded into the corridor outside the door. Many were dressed in fancy and expensive outfits, probably fresh from the *Star of Wonder*'s formal late-night activities. Others were dressed more haphazardly, as if they'd been asleep and had just thrown on whatever was handy. Still others were wearing the neat but simple clothing of servants or bodyguards.

All of them looked anxious. Most of them looked angry.

Facing them down, his back pressed against the door, was a security man wearing a sergeant's shoulder patches. "I appreciate your concerns, ladies and gentlemen," the sergeant was saying as Jack joined the back of the crowd. "Our investigation of the room is proceeding as quickly as possible. When it's finished, you'll all be allowed to examine your individual deposit boxes."

He held up his hand as several voices tried to speak at once. "However, I can assure you right now that you almost certainly have nothing to worry about. At the moment, it appears that no one actually got into the vault."

"Then what set off the security alarm?" someone demanded. "I heard it right through the ballroom wall."

"And the captain told *me* that the vault *had* been opened," someone else added.

"That was the first report, yes," the sergeant conceded. "However, it appears now that it was a false alarm. The lock does not seem to have been tampered with, and no one entered any codes into it. We're doing an electronic confirmation of that now."

"Yes, but—"

Behind the sergeant the door opened and another security man appeared. The two of them talked together for a minute in low voices as a buzz of conversation rippled through the crowd.

The sergeant turned back. "I've just been informed that the lock pad has definitely not been tampered with," he said. "We can therefore assume that the door indicator was indeed a false alarm."

Jack smiled to himself. Security knew perfectly well that there was more to it than that, of course. The smoke bomb in the monitor room vent and the knife he'd put through the camera junction box proved that much, not to mention the unlocked office door. Someone in authority must have decided to downplay the whole thing so as not to worry the passengers any more than necessary.

To be fair, of course, the sergeant was certainly right on one point. The lock pad *hadn't* been tampered with.

"Lieutenant Snyder has also informed me that we'll be allowing you in now to check your boxes," he went on. "If you'll all wait out here, we'll take you in one at a time."

"How about we wait *in*side?" someone demanded.

"That's right," another voice put in. "I want to know if *anybody* lost anything."

A chorus of agreement ran around the crowd. "Very well," the sergeant said, giving in. "Follow me, please. And make sure you have your keys ready."

One by one, they were brought behind the counter. Each person gave his or her box number, showed some identification, and was allowed into the vault to confirm everything was in order. Then, satisfied if not exactly happy, they wandered off back to their staterooms or their interrupted evening's entertainment.

At least, most of them did.

The man who'd checked out Box 125 was one of those dressed like servants or bodyguards. From his size and the way he walked, Jack had quickly narrowed that down to bodyguard.

Following at a careful distance, he tracked the other to what Uncle Virgil would have called "crust central," the most expensive section of the starliner's living sections. The door he went into was at the far end of one of the more luxurious corridors.

"The top of the top," Jack commented as they headed back toward the more modest area where his own stateroom was located.

"Pardon?" Draycos asked.

"A room at the end of a corridor like that is probably a suite," Jack explained. "Something the size of the *Essenay*, I'd guess. Probably costs more per week than the *Star of Wonder*'s captain makes in a year. High-level corporate territory, all right."

"A likely target for a human such as Cornelius Braxton, then?"

"Very much so," Jack agreed. "Guys like Braxton prefer to go for big bites instead of little nibbles." He jerked his thumb back in the direction of the suite. "Whoever's in there is definitely in the big-bite category."

Draycos was silent a moment. "Then let us hope that Braxton has bitten off more than he can swallow."

Jack glanced down at the dragon in surprise. "Hey, that's a human saying," he commented. "Where did you pick it up?"

"It is also K'da wisdom," Draycos told him. "Perhaps the thought is universal."

"Could be," Jack said. "Yes, let's hope this guy sticks in his throat."

"When will we speak to him?"

"There's no point trying to barge in tonight," Jack said. "We'll let him sleep in and try to see him in the morning."

"What will you do with the cylinder?"

"I thought you were the one who wanted to give it back," Jack reminded him.

"But we do not want to bring it with us to his room," Draycos pointed out. "That would leave no room for conversation."

"Yeah, you're right," Jack agreed, chewing his lip. "No

room for bargaining, either. He'd just whistle for the captain and have me thrown in the brig."

"We also do not want the humans from the *Advocatus Diaboli* to find it," Draycos added.

"Right," Jack said. "And we know they're aboard somewhere."

"We must therefore find a hiding place," Draycos concluded.

Ahead was a bank of elevators. "No problem," Jack assured him. "Watch the master and learn."

He touched the call button and the rightmost elevator door slid open. Jack stepped inside and pushed for the lowest deck. "Lowest deck is vehicle storage," he told Draycos as the doors slid closed. "A thousand places to hide something this size. Especially if anyone watching me notices that I've gone down there."

"You will hide it in a vehicle, then?"

"Like I said, watch the master," Jack said, pulling the cylinder from his inside coat pocket. "You know, we really ought to mark this thing somehow, in case it ever gets mixed up with the fake one. Let's see . . ."

With a bound, Draycos leaped out from his collar and landed beside him. "Permit me," he said, holding up one of his front paws. "Hold it firmly with the end facing me, please."

Frowning, Jack did so. The dragon extended a claw and scraped it briefly against the bottom of the cylinder. "There," he said.

Jack turned the cylinder around to look. Sure enough, there was a subtle but quite visible symbol scratched into the metal. "It is *kesh*," Draycos identified it. "The first letter in the K'da word for *genuine*."

Jack whistled softly. "So those claws of yours cut right through metal, huh?"

"Certain metals, yes," Draycos said, "though the harder varieties require more effort than a soft metal like this one." He cocked his head. "Why? Does that disturb you?"

Jack shrugged uncomfortably. "It doesn't exactly fill me with warm fuzzies, if that's what you mean," he admitted, swinging open the elevator's trouble panel. Behind the panel was a recessed box containing an emergency phone. "Here, hold this," he added, handing the dragon the cylinder and pulling out his multitool. He set to work on the side panel of the phone box, unfastening two of the screws that held it in place.

"Does that mean it *does* disturb you?" Draycos asked again, gripping the cylinder between his front paws.

"A little, I guess," Jack said. He had the side panel loose enough to swing inward, exposing the wires and soft foam sound insulation packed in between the side of the phone box and the elevator wall. "I mean, let's face it. You K'da are superior to humans in about every way I can think of."

He took the cylinder back and pressed it into the insulation. It fit, barely. "You're faster, you're stronger, and you're probably smarter," he went on, pushing the panel back into place and starting to fasten the screws again. "You can turn two-dimensional and look through walls. And now I find out you can scratch metal, too. What *can't* you do?"

"We cannot live alone," Draycos said softly. "Not for longer than six hours."

Jack paused, frowning over his shoulder. The dragon was standing motionless, with no emotion that Jack could read on his long face. But at the same time, he could somehow sense a deep sadness there. "Yeah," he said. "There is that."

The beeping of the elevator as it passed the next floor reminded him that time was short. Turning back, he finished fastening the plate and swung the trouble panel door shut again. He was on his feet, putting the multitool away, when the elevator settled onto the deck he'd punched for.

A flicker of weight on his neck, and Draycos was again safely hidden away. The elevator doors started to open; and Jack settled into the earnest young boy act that had worked so well in the purser's office. There would be a guard around here somewhere. . . .

"Wow!" he said, stepping out of the elevator and looking around. Ahead, stretching as far as he could see, were rows and rows of cars and small aircraft.

There was a guard, all right: a man in white sitting in a booth just beside the elevators. "May I help you?" he asked.

"Oh, no, I just came down to see the cars," Jack said, trying to look friendly, startled, and harmless all at the same time. "My dad told me there were Rolls Royce-Dymeis here and everything."

"There sure are," the guard said. "But I'm afraid you can't just wander around. Do you have a vehicle of your own down here?"

"No," Jack said, letting his face fall a little.

The guard smiled sympathetically. "Sorry."

"Yeah," Jack said. "Thanks anyway."

He got back into the elevator and punched for his stateroom's level. "And that's that," he said as the elevator started up. "Anyone following my movements will figure I stashed the cylinder somewhere down there."

"You were not there long enough to do that," Draycos pointed out.

"Of course not," Jack said, smiling tightly. "But don't forget, they think Uncle Virgil is here, too. They'll figure I passed it off to him."

"I see." The dragon gave an odd sound, like a heavy rain splashing into a puddle. A chuckle? "There is at least one area where you humans excel. You are by far more clever than the K'da."

Jack made a face. "Yeah. Big fat furry deal."

They had reached their floor before Draycos spoke again. "You need not fear us, Jack," he said quietly as Jack stepped out of the elevator. "By the very nature of our limitation the K'da can only be friends, or companions, or servants. We can never be masters."

"Maybe," Jack said. "But our history's full of servants who decided they wanted to be the masters for a change. Usually, things got pretty unpleasant."

He shook his head. "But we didn't come here to discuss history. Let's get some sleep, huh? Tomorrow's going to be another real busy day."

CHAPTER 22

The luxury corridor was deserted the next morning as Jack made his way along it, his feet dragging through the thick carpet. Back in his own area, most people had already been up and about. The idle rich must like to sleep in.

"What will we do?" Draycos murmured.

Jack hunched his shoulders, glancing around at the hand-carved designs along the corridor walls. He'd traded in the fancy clothes he'd worn yesterday in favor of his usual jeans and leather jacket, and was definitely regretting that decision. He felt out of place enough even out here in the corridor. How much worse was he going to feel once he was actually in the suite down there at the end?

Assuming, of course, he actually got inside. "We do it straight," he murmured back as he reached the door. "Just walk up and push the buzzer."

He got to the door and reached for the buzzer. As he did so, there was the sound of sliding doors behind him.

He turned. Standing in the corridor, outside the two doors he'd just passed, were two large men. Both were dressed the same way as the bodyguard from last night, and both were looking steadily at him.

Jack let his hand fall to his side. "Or not," he added.

"Can we help you?" one of the men said as they both walked toward him.

"My name's Jack Morgan," Jack said, fighting against the sudden urge to duck between them and run away as fast as he could. There was an air of police or ex-police about both these men that was stirring all the old reflexes. "I'd like to speak with your boss."

"May I ask your business?" the first man said as they reached him. They were, he noted, somewhat bigger than they had first looked.

"I have something that belongs to him," Jack said. "I'd like to arrange for its return."

The second man had pulled out a small scanner and was running it down Jack's chest. "Really," the first man said, a slight frown wrinkling his forehead. "What is it?"

Jack shook his head. "Sorry. Confidential."

"That's okay," the first man said, giving Jack what was probably his best effort at a friendly smile. "He doesn't have any secrets from us."

Jack lifted his eyebrows. "Really. A man in his position, and no secrets at all from his bodyguards? That's amazing."

The smile vanished. "Look, kid—"

"He's clean," the second man announced, putting the scanner away inside his jacket and tapping the comm clip on his collar. "Boyle?"

"Right here," a voice answered faintly from the clip. "What is it, Harper?"

"We've got a kid out here named Jack Morgan who wants

to see The Man," Harper said. "Says he has something that belongs to him."

"Does he?"

"Not on him," Harper said. "You want to check with him?"

The other voice snorted. "What, over some con artist running a scam?"

"I told you, he's just a kid," Harper said. "Twelve, thirteen, maybe."

"So it's a junior scam," Boyle said. "I'm not going to disturb The Man for this."

"I'm already disturbed, Boyle," a new, fainter voice came from the comm clip. "Have them send him in."

"Yes, sir," Harper said, his voice suddenly more respectful. He touched the comm clip again and gestured Jack toward the door. "You heard him. Go on in."

"Thanks," Jack said, frowning as he turned back to the door. There had been something familiar about that second comm clip voice. . . .

The door slid open as he stepped toward it. Taking a deep breath, painfully aware of Harper and his friend blocking his escape route behind him, he stepped inside.

He found himself in a room about half the size of the entire *Essenay,* and every bit as luxurious as he'd guessed it would be. The carved-wood walls were covered with paintings and embedded light-sculptures, the furniture was heavy and expensive looking, and the carpet was thick enough to hide large rodents in. Two archways led off to other parts of the suite, one of them from the right-hand side of the room, the other from the back.

Seated behind a computer at a desk to the left of the door,

scowling up at Jack, was a young man. A cup of something steaming sat on the desk to his right, a neat row of data tubes to his left. His clothes, Jack noted, were a couple of notches above the outfits the guards out in the corridor were wearing. That probably made him a secretary or assistant.

On the other side of the door sat another bodyguard type. Unlike the men outside, this one had his jacket off, showing the shoulder holster he was wearing under his left arm. He was pretending to read a newssheet, but Jack could tell that was just an act. One suspicious move on Jack's part, and that gun could be out of its holster in half a heartbeat.

"You Morgan?" the secretary type demanded. His voice, Jack noted, was the one that had first answered the guard outside.

"Yes," Jack said, turning to face him. "You must be Mr. Boyle."

"This had better be important, kid," Boyle growled. "And if you try to swing some gribble on me, you're going to regret it. What's so funny?"

"Sorry," Jack apologized, wiping away his smile. "It's just amusing when one of you corporate types tries to use street slang."

Boyle scowled a little harder. "So what's this about?"

Jack shook his head. "Like I told your friends outside, I need to talk directly to your boss."

"Not a chance," Boyle said. "You tell me. If *I* think it's worth his time, *I'll* tell him about it."

Jack crossed his arms. "His merchandise," he said flatly. "His ear. Or he doesn't get it back."

Boyle stood up, leaning his palms on the desktop and looking Jack straight in the eye. "Last chance," he warned.

Jack hesitated. Maybe he *shouldn't* expect to get in this easily. No one here knew him, after all. "I'll tell you this much," he said. "It has to do with the number four-oh-seven-six-six-two. Tell him that, and see if he wants to see me."

Boyle's lips pressed together in a thin line. "And what's that supposed to mean?"

"He'll know," Jack assured him. "No one else needs to."

Boyle's gaze shifted over Jack's shoulder to the bodyguard. "Vance? Toss him out."

"Just a moment," another voice came from the back archway. It was the second voice Jack had heard over Harper's comm clip.

He turned. The man standing in the archway was fully dressed in a casual but expensive suit. No sleeping in late for him, obviously. His face was in shadow, but there was enough light coming from the room behind him to show that his brown hair had streaks of white in it. An old man, then, the sort who would have had a lifetime to build up a business empire of his own. Exactly the sort of person Cornelius Braxton might be trying to take down. "I'm here, Mr. Morgan," the old man said. "You have one minute to make your point."

Jack took a deep breath. This was it. "Then I'll be brief," he said. "I believe that Cornelius Braxton of Braxton Universis is making a move against you. A scheme that involves the cylinder you think you've got locked away in Box 125 in the purser's safe."

The man's head cocked slightly to the side. "That I 'think' I have locked away?"

"Yes, sir," Jack said. "The one in there is a duplicate. I have the original."

"That's ridiculous," Boyle insisted. "Carpenter checked it just last night—"

"That will be all, Boyle," the old man said. His voice was calm but cool, not giving anything away. Jack wished he could see the expression on his face. "Are you telling me you took it, Mr. Morgan? In and out of the purser's safe without being caught?"

"Well, I had some help," Jack admitted. "And I didn't want to do it at all. Braxton blackmailed me into the job."

"How?"

"His men tried to frame me for theft," Jack said. "When that didn't work, they upped the ante and framed me for murder. Look, the point is that I've got the cylinder, and that I want to give it back."

"After going to all the trouble to steal it? Why?"

That whole conversation with Draycos flashed through Jack's mind: warrior ethics, looking out for yourself, doing what was right simply because it *was* right. It seemed way too complicated to go into here in the middle of crust central.

Besides, Jack wasn't sure himself any more why he was doing this. "Because whatever's going on, Braxton is up to something underhanded," he said, settling for the easiest of the possible answers. "I don't think he should get away with it, that's all."

"An interesting story," the man said. Stirring, he stepped forward out of the shadow of the archway, and Jack got his first clear look at his face.

He was old, all right, maybe even fifty. His face had some lines and a few wrinkles, a lot of them set around his sparkling blue eyes. The white-streaked brown hair Jack had already noted was matched by a neatly trimmed white-speckled brown beard.

And like the voice, the face seemed oddly familiar. Jack frowned, trying to remember where he'd seen it before. The newssheets? Television? The VideoNets?

"There's only one small problem with it," the old man continued, still walking toward Jack.

Suddenly, like a crack of thunder in the back of Jack's head, it clicked.

And as it did, his whole theory of what was going on here shattered into a thousand pieces.

"Because, you see," the old man said, "I *am* Cornelius Braxton."

For a moment Jack couldn't speak, his mouth hanging open in stunned bewilderment. "Mr. Braxton," he managed at last. "But . . ."

"I see you do recognize me," Braxton said. "Now, do you wish to continue your story? Or shall I have Vance throw you out?"

Jack shook his head, trying to get his brain to stop spinning. What in the name of vacuum sealant was going *on*? "I'm sorry, Mr. Braxton," he said. "But I'm very confused here. That phony theft, the one I told you they first tried to frame me for? That was with a Braxton Universis cargo on Vagran."

"My cargoes travel all over the Orion Arm," Braxton reminded him. "You need more than that."

"And then they took me aboard a Braxton Universis ship," Jack said. "The *Advocatus Diaboli*. The guy aboard—"

He stopped as something flickered on the man's face. "The *Advocatus Diaboli*?" Braxton repeated. "Are you sure?"

"Positive," Jack said. "My companion saw it and took down the name—"

"*Blast* it!" Boyle bit out. "Vance—cover them!"

Jack jumped, twisting to his right as he caught the sudden movement out of the corner of his eye. The guard was on his feet, his newssheet crumpled on the floor.

His gun pointed straight at Jack.

"Wait a second," Jack protested, his mouth suddenly dry. What had he said? "Look, Mr. Braxton—"

"Shut up!" Boyle snapped. "Lieutenant! Get in here! Quick!"

"You stupid fool," another familiar voice snarled from the side archway. "Do I have to do everything myself?"

Jack turned to look . . . and felt his breath catch in his throat.

It was Lieutenant Raven.

CHAPTER 23

Jack stared at Raven, his head spinning. No—this couldn't be happening.

"The *Advocatus Diaboli,* you say?" Braxton commented quietly.

With an effort, Jack tore his eyes away from Raven and looked back at Braxton. First Raven, and now Braxton, too. It was like one of those awful times back with Uncle Virgil and his friends when someone pulled a joke and everyone was in on it. Everyone, that is, except Jack. He would think something was happening, something important or dangerous or scary.

Then someone would laugh, and then everyone would laugh, and he'd realize they were all laughing at him.

He took a good look at Braxton's face. If this was a joke, Braxton wasn't in on it, either.

And no one in the room was laughing.

"Put your hands up, Mr. Braxton," Raven ordered, drawing his gun as he strode toward them across the room. "Blast it all, Boyle. Of all the flat-headed, idiotic—"

"But he knows," Boyle protested, jabbing a finger at Jack.

"He knows everything. The ship, Mr. Neverlin—"

"So he knows," Raven snapped, glaring at the secretary. "So you sit here and pick his story apart and pretend he's blowing smoke."

"But—"

"You blew it, Boyle," Raven cut him off. "You panicked and you blew it. Now we've got a real mess to clean up."

He stepped behind Braxton and stuck his gun into the older man's back. With his free hand he patted Braxton's clothes, searching for weapons. Jack watched him, feeling like he was going to be sick. He'd tried to do what was right; and instead he'd landed smack in the middle of an even bigger pit than he'd been in before.

Because there was no doubt that he, Jack Morgan, was the mess Raven was talking about cleaning up. Him, and maybe Braxton. Two of them, by themselves, against Raven and his men. It was just like the old days, with him and Uncle Virgil going up against the cops or the system or even other criminals.

Only this time it was him and Cornelius Braxton. At least Uncle Virgil had known what he was doing in a con or a fight or a slink. You could count on him to have a trick or two up his sleeve.

But Braxton wasn't Uncle Virgil. He was old, and he was way out of his element here. He probably hadn't had a fight outside a corporate boardroom in thirty years. Jack's skin began to crawl with the thought.

He frowned in sudden realization. No; that wasn't *his* skin crawling.

It was Draycos.

In the flick of an eye his mood and his fear and all the old memories vanished away. Yes, it was like the old days, all right. Only this time it was *Jack* who had the trick up his sleeve.

Whatever Raven had in mind, Jack would bet heavy odds that it didn't include the possibility of a K'da poet–warrior joining the game.

He reached up and squeezed his shoulder, hoping Draycos would take the hint and stay put for now. Part of the reason Uncle Virgil had never been thrown in prison, he knew, was that the cops had never been able to gather enough evidence against him.

Before he turned his pet K'da loose on this gang, maybe he could get Raven to brag a little.

He looked back at Braxton. "So who's Mr. Neverlin?" he asked casually.

Raven threw a frown at Jack over Braxton's shoulder. "You're pretty calm," he said suspiciously. "You counting on your uncle to pull you out of this?"

"One of the benefits of a clear conscience," Jack assured him. "And, of course, the fact that I still have the cylinder."

Raven snorted. "Dream on, kid. Now that the plan has gone down in flames, I don't need it anymore."

"Oh," Jack said. "Well . . . in that case, would you mind telling me what the plan *was*?"

"Watch them," Raven ordered Boyle and Vance, stepping away from Braxton and heading back to the archway. "I'll be back in a minute."

"I think I can fill in the blanks, Mr. Morgan," Braxton said calmly. He might be old, Jack realized, but he was a long way from being out of his element. His face was clear and thoughtful, his eyes taking everything in. "The *Advocatus Diaboli* is assigned to the chairman of my board, Arthur Neverlin. I would say that he's decided he wants to run the whole company by himself."

"He already seems to be running some of your people," Jack said, inclining his head toward Boyle. "Where does the cylinder fit in?"

"It contains DNA samples taken from my wife and me when we were twenty," Braxton explained. "Every few years we take a month-long cruise like this, go to a clinic on Parsonia, and take rejuvenation treatments. The DNA is part of it."

He smiled. "I'm actually considerably older than I look."

"Ah," Jack said, nodding. The man must be ancient, then. "Must be something in the duplicate that'll kill you."

"No doubt," Braxton agreed. "But subtly, of course. Always very subtle, our Mr. Neverlin."

Jack looked around. "So where *is* your wife?"

"She's out walking on the promenade level." Braxton looked thoughtfully at Boyle. "I wonder if her guards are in on this, too."

Jack looked at Boyle, too. The man was standing silently, but his throat was working up and down. "Offhand, I'd say they aren't," he told Braxton.

"You shut up," Boyle snapped, clenching his teeth in Jack's direction. "*You* we don't have to find a clever way of getting rid of."

"Cork it, Boyle," Raven growled from across the room as he strode back in under the archway. With him was another guard. "Okay, Myers and I have a plan."

"Hope this one works better than the last one did," Jack murmured.

"I *could* just let Boyle take you off somewhere, you know," Raven said pointedly. "It wouldn't be nearly as painless a way to go."

"Never mind him," Boyle said. "What are we going to do about Mrs. Braxton? She could be back any minute."

"Forget her," Raven said. "She'll keep. What we have to do now is make Braxton disappear."

"What, here on the ship?" Boyle demanded. "Are you nuts?"

"Relax," Raven told him. "We're docking with Shotti Station in five hours for cargo pickup. If we can keep up the pretense that he's aboard until then, we can make it look like he got off there."

"And what exactly would I be doing at Shotti Station?" Braxton asked mildly.

Raven smiled tightly. "Meeting a special courier from Mr. Neverlin, of course."

"Ah," Braxton said. "And you already have this set up with him?"

"No," Raven said. "But we'll have plenty of time afterward to work out those details."

"After what?" Jack asked.

"After you two take a swim out the airlock," Raven said bluntly.

"An airlock?" Braxton said, lifting his eyebrows politely. "Really. That should be interesting."

"Don't get your hopes up," Raven warned, jerking his head toward the new guard. "Myers found a cargo lock that isn't guarded or watched. Bay AA-3. Should be nice and quiet."

"And you expect us to meekly walk in there?" Braxton asked. "Just like that?"

"Just like that," Raven nodded. "Because if you try to warn or alert anyone along the way, we'll kill them too. You don't want to go to your death with someone else's life on your conscience, do you?"

Braxton didn't answer. But his face seemed to sag, just a little. "I didn't think so," Raven said, shifting his gaze to Jack. "How about you?"

"Oh, I'll cooperate," Jack said. "But I think there's something else you've forgotten."

"Who, your uncle?" Raven said with a sniff. "Don't flatter yourself. I met Virgil Morgan once. He's not going to stick his neck into trouble for you. Either of you."

He pointed a finger at Jack. "But don't take it personally. After we're finished with you, we'll track him down."

Jack pursed his lips. "I wish you luck," he said. "He won't be easy to find."

"We'll find him," Raven promised. "Trust me."

He drew his gun from its holster and slipped it and his hand into the side pocket of his coat. "Boyle, you stay here and deal with the wife when she comes back. Nothing fancy—tell her he's gone for a stroll. Vance, Myers, you're coming with us."

He gestured toward the door. "Mr. Braxton? After you."

CHAPTER 24

With Vance in the lead, Braxton, Jack, and Raven behind him, and Myers bringing up the rear, they headed out.

The two guards Jack had run into earlier were still on the job, and they stepped out of their rooms as the parade came by. Jack held his breath; but Braxton merely waved them back to their posts. Jack looked at their faces as he passed, but there was no suspicion there that he could see.

They might be suspicious later, of course. But by then it would be too late. Or so Raven probably hoped, anyway.

He might be right, too. True, Jack still had Draycos hidden away. But even under ideal conditions it would still be three armed men against a single unarmed K'da.

And the conditions here were anything but ideal. Raven walked close behind Braxton and Jack as they made their way along, his gun pressing through his coat into Braxton's back whenever someone came close. Draycos could easily take him out, probably before the man even knew what had hit him.

But Vance and Myers were keeping their distance. No matter how fast he was, the dragon could never get to both of them before the shooting started.

The group was soon out of the high-class living section and into the *Star of Wonder*'s main eating and entertainment area. More and more people were milling around here, and Jack waited expectantly for Vance and Myers to close the gap between them. Surely they would want to prevent any chance of Braxton or Jack darting off and losing themselves in the crowds.

But they still kept their distance. It was almost as if they were expecting an attack . . . and it wasn't until the group had passed the central elevator bank that Jack suddenly realized that that was exactly what they *were* expecting. Not from a hidden K'da warrior, of course, but from Uncle Virgil.

Back in Braxton's suite, dropping all those vague hints and threats had seemed like a clever thing to do. Now, Jack wasn't so sure about that.

"We'll be passing the casino soon," Braxton murmured from beside him. "That may be your best hope."

For a couple of steps Jack was strongly tempted. Raven's gun was stuck in Braxton's back, after all, not his. If he could make it into the casino, there were all those game tables and chance machines for him to duck and dodge among. There were bound to be security people on duty there, too.

But there were still Vance and Myers to think about. Braxton didn't seem the type to hire bodyguards who couldn't shoot straight. "Thanks for the offer," he murmured back. "But I think I'll stick it out."

"They're going to kill me, Jack," Braxton reminded him. "As Raven said, I really don't want to die with other lives on my conscience."

Jack frowned sideways at him. Braxton's face was set in hard lines; but at the same time Jack could tell that the man meant it.

It seemed a far cry from the hard, cold, merciless industrial giant that everyone thought of when Cornelius Braxton's name was mentioned. Maybe Braxton was rearranging his way of thinking now that he could see his own death approaching.

Or maybe the public image wasn't what the man was really like at all.

"It's okay," he told Braxton. "And don't give up hope. Not yet."

Braxton glanced around. "All right," he said. "If you say so."

"Over here," Raven said, taking Braxton's shoulder and guiding him into a right-hand turn. They went through a door with the now familiar—at least to Jack—*Authorized Personnel Only* sign on it. A short corridor away, they reached a large elevator door.

"Say good-bye to civilization," Raven advised as the elevator doors slid open. "Next stop'll be the cargo section."

Jack had held out some hope that in the confined space of an elevator car Draycos would finally have a chance to act. But accidentally or otherwise, Raven had neatly squashed that one. The car he ushered them into wasn't one of the regular passenger elevators, but instead a cargo lift. It was nearly the size of Jack's stateroom, and Vance and Myers went immediately to opposite corners.

Raven stepped well back, too. Now that secrecy wasn't important anymore, all three men drew their guns out of hiding. Myers touched the button, and the car started down.

"Jack?" a voice murmured in Jack's right ear.

Jack measured the distances with his eyes. Too far. Besides, there was no cover anywhere for him and Braxton to duck behind when the shooting started. "Not here," he murmured back, keeping his lips motionless.

"We are running out of time," Draycos pointed out.

"Don't you think I know that?" Jack retorted quietly. "It just won't work in here."

"Hey," Myers said, jabbing his gun toward Jack. "Did anyone think to check this clown for a comm clip?"

"Harper ran him," Raven told him. "He was clean."

"Then who's he talking to?" Myers demanded. "Maybe I ought to do a little more *thorough* search, if you know what I mean."

"He was talking to me," Braxton spoke up. "Is that a problem?"

"What about?" Myers asked.

"None of your business," Braxton said calmly. "Most condemned men are allowed a last meal. You should at least be gracious enough to allow us a last conversation."

"Yeah?" Myers growled, starting forward. "Maybe we're not feeling gracious today, huh?"

"It's all right, Myers," Raven said, waving the other back. "Let them talk."

Myers glared some more, but he returned to his corner without argument. "Thanks," Jack murmured to Braxton.

Braxton nodded, his eyes on Raven. "You know, Mr. Raven, there's no reason you have to kill our young friend here," he commented. "There are several techniques that can be used to block his memories of this entire trip."

"Sorry," Raven said, shaking his head. "I know all about those techniques. I don't trust any of them."

"I could make it worth your while," Braxton offered.

Raven grinned evilly. "Thanks, but I think Mr. Neverlin

already has enough of the pie to outbid you. He sure will after today."

"This is an account Neverlin doesn't know about," Braxton persisted. "One he'll never find on his own. A little extra money never hurt anyone."

"A little extra loose end can hurt plenty," Raven retorted. "Now shut up."

Braxton looked at the other two. "Myers? Vance? Either of you interested?"

"I said *shut up!*" Raven snarled, gesturing with his gun. "Or I'll drop you right here."

Braxton gave up. The rest of the elevator ride was made in silence.

The doors opened onto a corridor that was clearly one of the ship's working areas. No fancy carvings or carpeting or even textured wall coverings here. Everything was plain synth-wall and scuffless flooring, with wires and conduits running in plain sight along the ceilings.

It was better than a lot of places Jack had been in. Still, coming from the fancier parts of the liner, it seemed shockingly bleak and shabby. A very depressing place to have to die in.

Raven was obviously thinking the same thing. "Sorry about the decor," he said as Vance led them around a corner into a cross-corridor. "I would have ordered flowers, only you weren't supposed to go down for another couple of weeks."

"You didn't get any flowers for those Wistawki, either," Jack murmured. If he was going to get Raven to confess to the murders, this was the time for it. "The ones you shot on Vagran. You didn't seem to care at all about them, in fact."

Raven snorted. "What, get misty-eyed over a bunch of dumb animals? Who cares if a couple of them get shot?"

"You thought enough people would care to make it worth framing me for their murders," Jack reminded him.

"I probably still will, too," Raven said with a shrug. "Might as well get that off the books, and you're as good a fall guy as anyone. Especially since you won't be around to tell your side of it."

"Unless Drabs turns on you," Jack pointed out.

"Don't worry, Drabs knows what side of the bread gets the butter," Raven assured him.

"Maybe," Jack said. "But like you, he was willing to stab Mr. Braxton in the back. Maybe he'll do the same to you if he gets the chance."

Raven snorted. "Nice try. I can handle Drabs."

"Well, then, maybe the Brummga will turn," Jack said. "He was a witness, too, remember."

"A Brummga?" Braxton asked, frowning. "There aren't any Brummgas in my security force."

"You know, kid, you talk way too much," Raven growled. "How about you shut up for the rest of the trip?"

Jack sighed. "Sure."

Three minutes and two corridors later, they reached the cargo hold.

Like everything else on the *Star of Wonder,* it was a pretty impressive place. It was big, for starters, built more along the lines of a warehouse than a simple storage room. The ceiling was high, maybe twenty feet up, with a grid of lifter-crane rails crisscrossing it and at least three heavy-duty cranes riding them. Hanging a few feet below the ceiling between the rails was another grid, this one a network of service catwalks. Rows of lights set into the ceiling made the room almost as bright as day.

Over the door they'd entered by, and clustered together into four more groups in different parts of the ceiling, were the familiar battery-equipped emergency lights. There were, unfortunately, almost certainly no security cameras hidden inside them as there had been in those in the purser's office.

Stacked neatly on the well-lit floor were piles of crates, protected by acceleration webbing, with open aisles between them. All of the stacks were too tall to see over; most of them reached nearly to the catwalks overhead.

It reminded Jack of the Vagran spaceport, and for that first hopeful moment he wondered if he might be lucky enough for the cargo to be laid out in the same sort of maze. If it was, and if he and Braxton could get just a few seconds ahead of their captors, they might at least have a chance of making a game of hide-and-seek out of this.

But then he got a second glance, and the brief hope melted away. The Vagran warehouse floor had been laid out in randomly sized rectangles, which was what had accounted for the crooked walkways. Here, though, the rectangles were all the same size, with the aisles between them as straight as Parprin city streets. Anyone trying to escape down one of them would be shot in the back before he got fifteen feet.

Unless they didn't know anyone had escaped. . . .

"Nice," he commented, looking around. "A lot roomier than my place upstairs."

"Glad you like it," Raven said. "Myers, where's this airlock?"

"Far side," Myers said, gesturing straight ahead with his gun. "Maybe a little to the right."

"Okay, you take point," Raven said, nudging Braxton forward. "Move. And remember to keep quiet if you don't want us burning innocent bystanders."

The aisles were just wide enough for two people to walk comfortably side by side. With Myers in the lead and Vance now bringing up the rear, the group headed in.

Quietly, Jack reached down to his right jacket cuff and casually unsnapped it. The last time Draycos had tried to go out that way through the jacket, he'd nearly broken Jack's wrist. He just hoped the dragon would remember that, and pick up on the hint.

He did. Jack could feel him sliding along his body, easing as much of himself as he could onto Jack's right arm, getting ready to spring.

"Easy," Jack muttered. "You'll know when."

Ahead, they were coming up on one of the cross aisles. Jack took a deep breath, watching Myers's back and counting his own steps. This was going to take some careful timing if he didn't want to get himself shot.

Myers walked past the cross aisle, glancing both ways as he passed it, and continued on. Jack focused on the aisle, estimating how many steps ahead of him it was. Three, he decided, would be the magic number. When he was three steps away, he would go.

Five steps away.

Four.

Three.

Jumping away from Braxton's side, he sprinted forward.

The move caught everyone by surprise. He'd made it one step before Raven even got out a startled curse; two steps before Myers started to twist back around; three steps before he heard the sound of Braxton being shoved aside as Raven tried to bring his gun to bear.

And then he was at the cross aisle. Leaning his weight to the left, he threw himself hard into it.

Threw himself a little too hard, in fact. As he tried to make the turn his feet skidded out from under him. He grabbed for the side of the nearest stack of crates, missed, and toppled over hard onto his side. From the aisle he'd just left, the aisle his feet were still sticking out into, came the sound of curses and orders as Raven and his men scrambled to catch up with him. Two seconds, maybe, and they would be on top of him.

But for those precious two seconds, the top half of his body was out of their sight.

Draycos came out of the end of Jack's right sleeve like a black thundercloud twisting over a prairie town. He caught the webbing on the side of the stack with his claws and skittered up the side. By the time Raven and Myers spun madly around the corner, he had vanished over the top.

"You little snot," Raven snarled viciously, grabbing Jack by the front of his jacket and hauling him up onto his feet. Before Jack could get his balance, the man slammed him up against the stack of crates. "I ought to kill you right here," he threatened, his face three inches from Jack's, the muzzle of his gun jammed hard into Jack's stomach. "I ought to burn your fingers off, then kill you right here."

"You start burning me and I probably won't be able to keep from screaming," Jack said, his voice trembling with reaction. "Someone might hear. How many people can you toss out an airlock before people start wondering where they all went?"

For a long, terrifying moment he thought Raven was going to decide he didn't care. But even seething with anger, he could apparently see the reason in that. Slowly, reluctantly, he moved back. "Vance?"

Vance appeared, his gun pressed warningly into the back of Braxton's neck. "Yeah?"

"You stay on Braxton," Raven ordered. "I'll take the kid personally. Let's go."

Jack took a deep breath as they all moved back into the aisle and continued on their way. He had done all that he could.

Now it was up to Draycos.

CHAPTER 25

Draycos leaped from Jack's sleeve as high as he could. His out-stretched claws caught the side of the boxes, and the netting that held them in place. The netting was a perfect grip, and he ran up the side of the stack, going nearly as fast as he could have on flat ground.

He scrambled over the edge onto the top, and immediately twisted around to cautiously look down.

The caution wasn't necessary. The three humans below weren't looking around for him, but had eyes only for Jack and Braxton. Most likely, they were completely unaware of what had just taken place.

He pulled back from the edge, giving the room a quick look. There was a series of narrow walkways hanging from the ceiling above him. He leaped to the nearest of them, managing to get over the safety railing and onto the walkway itself with-out making any noise. Keeping his claws withdrawn, running silently on the soft pads of his paws, he headed back toward the door they'd come in through.

Twice now Jack had stopped him when he was preparing for action. The first time, two Wistawki had died because of it. The second time, up in Braxton's suite, he would probably have succeeded.

But at a cost that he now realized could have been disastrous. Because there was more at stake here than Braxton's life. More even than Jack's life, and that was saying a great deal. Jack was his host, and there was a high debt of honor between a K'da warrior and his host.

But even that honor could not balance against the lives of the entire K'da race. The human who had spoken to Jack aboard the *Advocatus Diaboli* had been part of the plot against his people; and whether Cornelius Braxton himself was part of it or not, it was likely that some of those around him were.

Which meant he could not permit Braxton to know of his existence.

Even if it cost Jack his life?

Draycos felt a knife-point of guilt digging beneath his scales as he raced along the hanging walkway toward the door. What had Jack intended him to do just now, he wondered? Had he expected him to leap onto Raven and the others as they came around the corner?

Because he could have done exactly that. Jack's risky break for freedom had startled the enemy into carelessness, causing them to bunch together. He could have taken all three of them without trouble. Probably before any of them had even known they were under attack.

But then Braxton would have seen him. And if he had, the K'da race might have died.

So instead Draycos had hidden out of sight on top of the boxes. Jack had been recaptured, and would now suffer whatever punishment Raven demanded for his action.

Soon, perhaps, he would die.

What did Jack think Draycos was doing now? Did he think Draycos was preparing a trap? Did he expect to suddenly have a K'da warrior drop into their midst, slashing and clawing?

Or did he think Draycos might be running away?

Thoughts of Uncle Virgil flickered through Draycos's mind. Uncle Virgil, and his ghostly echo inside the *Essenay*'s computer. That human had taught Jack to think only about himself, to do only that which benefited him. Was the boy even capable of thinking about higher things? Would he understand the idea of sacrificing something you valued, or someone you cared about, for something even more valuable?

Even if he did, would he think the K'da and Shontine worth the sacrifice of his life?

Probably not. Given time, Draycos knew he could teach the boy about such things as honor and integrity and justice. Jack had the potential to stand with the very finest of the K'da and Shontine.

But he wasn't there yet. Would he be able to find the strength to calmly die so that the K'da and Shontine might live? Draycos didn't think so.

But if he did his job right, neither of them would have to find out.

He reached the end of the walkway above the door. Fastened to the wall just below the ceiling was his target: the now-familiar square box of an emergency lighting system. From the battery pack a thick wire rose to each of the system's two lights. Two quick slashes of his claws, and the wires were cut.

He spun around on the walkway and headed back. There were four other clusters of emergency lights on the ceiling, each of the groups arranged in a circle with the lights facing outward. Moving along the grid, he made his way to each cluster in turn. Slashing systematically at the wires, he quickly disabled them.

And with that, everything was ready. He headed for the far end of the room, hoping he would be in time.

The sound of the humans' footsteps had stopped, but his view of them was still blocked. He sped along the walkway, blood tingling through his muscles and scales with his fear of what he would see. He passed the last stack of boxes and looked down.

The humans had reached the far wall and were standing near a heavy door with a control panel and status board beside it. Jack and Braxton stood together with their backs to the wall near the door. Raven stood facing them, his weapon pointed at Braxton. Vance stood a few paces away in guard position, his weapon also ready, while Myers worked at the control panel.

Draycos slowed to a silent trot, studying the lights overhead as he moved toward the humans. The power wires weren't buried inside an outer wall, as they were in the public areas of the ship, but were merely fastened in plain sight against the ceiling.

He wondered how much electrical power those wires contained. But it didn't really matter. Whatever was necessary, he would do it.

Below him, the airlock door swung open. "This is it," Raven said. "Get in."

Braxton took a step toward the door. Jack didn't move. "What, already?" the boy asked. "No chance for last words? A blindfold? Anything?"

Raven stepped over to him. Draycos couldn't see the human's expression, but his voice was suddenly vicious as he pressed his weapon into Jack's throat. "I hear death by asphyxiation isn't a bad way to go," he bit out. "Death by laser *is*. Now get *in*."

Jack still didn't move. "I think you're forgetting one thing, Raven. Mr. Braxton's DNA cylinder—well, the fake one, but you know what I mean. It's still in the purser's safe. If he disappears now, aren't they going to wonder why he didn't take it with him?"

Draycos smiled grimly. That was Jack, all right. Comments, complaints, objections, questions—the boy was stalling for time. Squeezing out every extra heartbeat he could to give his companion time to act.

And in that moment it occurred to Draycos that he could search far and wide throughout the Orion Arm and not find a better host and ally than he had in Jack Morgan.

He reached the end of the walkway. Jack and Braxton were almost directly below him now. "So he left the cylinder for his wife to use," Raven said with a snort. "We'll just make sure the story reads that he was planning to catch up with her on Parsonia."

"What about the fake cylinder?" Jack persisted. "Don't you think they'll find it a little suspicious that there are two of them?"

One of the power wires was directly over Draycos's head. Bracing himself, he lifted a paw and extended one of his claws.

"Who's going to know?" Raven countered. "Once we get your uncle, we'll have the other cylinder, too."

He put a hand on Jack's shoulder and shoved him roughly toward the airlock. "Now get *in*."

Jack's shoulders drooped in defeat. Taking a deep breath, he turned toward the door—

And with a defiant scream of the K'da battle cry, Draycos sliced through the power line. There was a brilliant spark, a flash-tingle of shock through his paw, and the entire room was plunged into darkness.

He was over the railing in an instant, dropping toward the floor below. In the faint light coming from the airlock control panel, he saw Raven spin around. Behind him, Jack grabbed Braxton's arm and pulled him to the floor. Vance and Myers had turned, too, their weapons swinging back and forth as they searched for a target. Unconsciously, perhaps, the three humans had pulled together into a semicircle, their backs toward the wall, facing outward.

Draycos dropped to the floor directly behind them.

Vance was first. Rising up on his hind legs, Draycos slammed his front paw hard against the side of the human's head. He dropped without even a gurgle, his weapon clattering across the floor.

There was a brief flash of light as Myers fired reflexively toward the noise. "Vance!" he yelped. "Raven—"

He never finished the sentence. Draycos was already behind him, and with another slash of his paw this second enemy also went flying.

Three shots burned through the air, one of them barely missing Draycos's left ear. He jumped aside to the right, hit the floor and immediately dodged left, each leap zigzagging him closer to Raven. The human was making wordless sounds, trying desperately to back away as he fired again and again at the black shadow bearing down on him.

But he couldn't back up nearly fast enough. Draycos made one final leap directly in front of him, batting his weapon out of his hand, then rising up on his hind paws to gaze directly into Raven's eyes.

In the dim reflected light he saw the look of terror on the human's face. Raven opened his mouth, to scream or shout or perhaps even to plead.

Draycos struck.

Not the disabling blows with which he had struck Vance and Myers. This was a much harder attack, aimed at Raven's neck instead of at the side of his head. Beneath his paw he felt the bone snap.

And Raven, the human who had killed two innocent Wistawki in cold blood, dropped to the floor, dead.

Across the room he could hear the sounds of commotion now, and between the stacks of cargo came the wavering glint of handheld lights. Leaving his vanquished enemies, he crossed to Jack's side.

The boy was lying protectively half on top of Braxton, keeping both of them flat on the floor. His arm and hand were placed across the side of the other human's head, positioned so that Braxton wouldn't be able to see what was happening.

Draycos smiled, flicking his tongue in admiration. Yes, he had indeed found a worthy partner.

The lights were getting closer, and there were anxious voices with them now. Stepping up behind Jack, Draycos put a paw on the back of his neck and melted back beneath his shirt onto his skin. "Jack?" he heard Braxton ask.

Jack let out a breath in relief, stretching his shoulders as Draycos settled into place. "It's okay," he told Braxton, patting the older human on the back and getting to his feet. "It's all over now."

CHAPTER 26

"More tea, dear?" Mrs. Braxton asked, holding the teapot poised over Jack's cup.

"Um," Jack said, remembering just in time that it wasn't polite to talk with your mouth full of food and possibly spray crumbs over everything. He shook his head instead, and concentrated on chewing. High tea, Mrs. Braxton had called this: a snack of hot tea and some kind of biscuit things she'd called scones. A weird name, but they tasted pretty good.

"Another scone, then?" she asked.

Again he shook his head. "Thanks, but I really ought to get going," he told her as he cleared his mouth enough to talk. "I've still got to pack, and we're due into Shotti Station pretty soon."

Actually, he had nothing to pack except the clothing he'd bought when he first came aboard the *Star of Wonder*. But he felt terribly uncomfortable here in Braxton's suite, and was anxious to get away.

Not that Braxton and his wife weren't being nice to him. The problem was, they were being too nice. Jack wasn't used to this kind of treatment, and three hours of it were just about all he could stand.

"I don't like leaving you here all alone like this," Mrs. Braxton said, setting the teapot down again. "Your uncle could be delayed, after all."

"No, it's okay," Jack said. "Really. If Uncle Virge said he'll meet me here, he will."

"Perhaps," Mrs. Braxton said, sounding doubtful. "Still, you've hardly even let us thank you for what you did. And now here you are running off again."

"The fuel credits Mr. Braxton gave me are all I need," Jack assured her, taking a sip of his tea. With enough sugar in it, this stuff was pretty good, too. "Anyway, I didn't do all that much."

"Come now," Mrs. Braxton said, lifting her eyebrows politely. "Don't be modest. You saved our lives and exposed a dangerous conspiracy within our company. Either of those alone would be worth far more than a few paltry fueling credits. Are you sure there isn't anything else we can do for you?"

You want to take a K'da warrior off my hands? Jack thought. But he just shook his head. "No, thanks," he said instead. "If Mr. Braxton can get that murder charge cleared away, we'll call it even."

"Then even it is," Braxton announced, coming in through one of the archways. "I've just spoken with the Vagran Police. It turns out that they came up with a witness to the murders. They showed him your reconstruction of how everyone was standing, and he confirmed that Raven was the one who fired the shots."

"That's good," Jack said, frowning. "What about Raven's photo? You *did* send a photo, didn't you?"

Braxton shrugged. "The witness was a Compfrin," he said. "They're not very good at picking out one human face from another. But the police say his testimony will be good enough."

Jack nodded. It wouldn't have been good enough for most of the police he and Uncle Virgil had locked horns with in the past, he knew. But on the other hand, if no one could identify Raven as the murderer, they couldn't very well finger him, either. It probably balanced out.

Especially with someone like Cornelius Braxton leaning on his end of the balance.

"We have an alert out for the *Advocatus Diaboli,* too," Braxton went on. "So far, no word."

"Do you suppose he's made a run for it?" Mrs. Braxton asked.

"I don't see him panicking this quickly," Braxton said. "Unless Raven failed to make a regular report, anyway. No, he's probably sitting off somewhere, rubbing his hands in anticipation of my death."

"Neverlin always did like to rub his hands together," Mrs. Braxton commented thoughtfully. "I never cared much for that."

"I've had a check made of our personnel files," Braxton said, pulling out one of the other chairs at the table and sitting down. "You're sure it was a Brummga you saw with Raven?"

"They're a little hard to miss," Jack reminded him.

"You're right about that," Braxton said, nodding. "Problem is, we don't have any Brummgas on our payroll, except for those working the plant on their home world. Certainly no one in a guard or security or executive assistant position."

"Perhaps Mr. Neverlin has picked up some allies," Mrs. Braxton suggested.

Jack thought back to the Brummga he'd run into aboard the wrecked *Havenseeker*. "Or else someone's picked *him* up as an ally," he murmured.

"What was that, dear?" Mrs. Braxton asked.

Jack shook his head. Sitting here like old friends or not, he still wasn't about to tell Braxton what he knew about the Iota Klestis ambush. Not yet, anyway. "Nothing," he said. "Just rambling."

Braxton reached over to the serving tray and picked up the cylinder Jack had set down there. "So this is the original?" he said, hefting it in his hand.

"Yes, sir," Jack said. "It's the one I got out of the purser's safe, anyway."

"You should probably mark it somehow, Neely," Mrs. Braxton said. "We wouldn't want to mix it up with the other one."

"I already did that," Jack told them. "That mark on the bottom. See?"

"Oh, yes," Braxton said, turning it over and peering at the bottom. "Yes. Very good. And you said you'll send that EvGa fingerprint data to me?"

"As soon as Uncle Virge gets here with the ship," Jack promised. "Those prints we got off the Vagran storage locker should help you pick out the rest of Neverlin's gang."

"Or at least some of them," Mrs. Braxton said.

"Either way, it will be useful," Braxton agreed. "Thank you again."

"No problem," Jack said, pushing back his chair and standing up. Just in time, he remembered to wipe his hands and mouth on the napkin beside his plate. "Well, unless there's something else, I'd better be going. Thanks for the hospitality."

"Thank you for our lives," Braxton said quietly, standing up beside him. Before Jack could realize what he was doing, the man reached out and shook his hand. "And we still owe you, Jack, whether you acknowledge that or not. If and when we can balance the scales, just let us know."

"I will," Jack promised. "Thanks for the tea and scones."

He was past the bodyguards and slogging his way through the luxury corridor's thick carpeting before he spoke again. "So tell me something," he said. "Was there any special reason why you knocked out Vance and Myers but broke Raven's neck?"

"Of course," Draycos answered from his shoulder. "Raven committed two intentional murders on Vagran. The punishment for such a crime is death. As a K'da warrior, it was both my right and my duty to pass judgment."

"Yeah, well, in the future try to sit on your sense of justice, okay?" Jack said. "You're in the Orion Arm now, and the cops here don't like people taking the law into their own hands."

"I understand," Draycos said. "It is clear that I still have a great deal to learn about your society. What will we do now?"

Jack shrugged. Uncle Virge wasn't going to be happy with this. But fair was fair. "We made a deal," he reminded the dragon. "You helped me with my problem. Now it's my turn to help you with yours. Let's go find out who hit your people."

"You are certain you are willing?" Draycos asked. "It may be a difficult path we will walk. Even if Braxton himself is not involved in the plot against my people, we are still facing one of his strongest lieutenants."

"Maybe," Jack said. "But I think Neverlin will have his hands pretty full for awhile keeping his head down. That ought to give us a little breathing space."

"Perhaps," Draycos said. "It is interesting, is it not, that people so often turn out to be different than we expect."

Jack snorted. "Don't fool yourself, kiddo. Braxton is still a hard-nosed businessman who'll do whatever it takes to get what he wants. We're just lucky that he happens to be on our side at the moment."

"That may indeed prove helpful," Draycos conceded. "Yet there will still be many other dangers facing us along the way."

Jack smiled. "What, me and my pet dragon? Bring 'em on."

The top of Draycos's head rose up from his shoulder to press against his shirt. "I am a poet-warrior of the K'da," he said, sounding offended. "I am *not* a pet dragon."

"Sure, sure," Jack soothed, patting him on his crest. "I know. Now keep your head down."

"I've sent word to all Braxton Universis plants and facilities, sir," Harper said, consulting his computer. "Ditto to the Internos Police, and I'm working on the various alien law enforcement bureaus. We should have the whole Orion Arm alerted within a few more days."

"Good," Braxton said, turning the cylinder over again in his hand and gazing at the curious design that had been scratched in the bottom. "When you're finished with that, call Anderson and have him start a full rundown on Jack Morgan. I want his history, his current occupation, family, friends—everything. Same goes for this Uncle Virge he mentioned."

"Yes, sir," Harper said, making a note.

"And after that, contact Chu and have him send a team to meet us on Parsonia," Braxton said. "I want to know what this symbol is that Jack carved here."

He handed the cylinder to his wife. "And," he added, "exactly what kind of tool he used to make it."

Look for

DRAGON
and SOLDIER

by **TIMOTHY ZAHN**

Available in Hardcover
June 2004

David Lubar

HIDDEN TALENTS

American Library Association
"Best Books for Young Adults"

"Wondrously surprising, playful, and heartwarming."—*VOYA*

"Sure to be popular."—*Kliatt*

Martin Anderson doesn't like being called a loser. But when he ends up at Edgeview Alternative School he has to face the truth: Edgeview is the end of the line. But he discovers something remarkable about himself and his friends: each has a special . . . *hidden* . . . talent.

IN THE LAND OF THE LAWN WEENIES
and other Misadventures

"Four stars!"—*Chicago Tribune*

"Really off the wall stories. They're funny thrillers that scare you out of your seat, but have you laughing all the time."
—Walter The Giant Storyteller

"Clever, creepy, and full of surprises."—James Howe

Kids can be *such* monsters. Literally. From the award-winning author of *Hidden Talents*, two remarkable short story collections—*Kidzilla* and *The Witch's Monkey*—together for the first time. Each hilarious and harrowing.

Orson Scott Card

ENDER'S GAME

Winner of the Hugo Award
Winner of the Nebula Award
An American Library Association
"100 Best Books for Teens"

Ender Wiggin has hardly had a childhood when representatives of the world government recruit him for military training at a facility called Battle School. A genius, Ender is considered a master strategist. His skills will be necessary if the Earth can repel another attack by alien Buggers. In simulated war games Ender excels. But how will he do in real battle conditions? After all, Battle School *is* just a game, right?

"Superb."—*Booklist*

ENDER'S SHADOW

2000 Alex Award Winner
An American Library Association
"Top 10 Best Book"

Life on the streets is tough. But if Bean has learned anything it's how to survive. Not with his fists. Bean is way too small to fight. But with his brain. Like his colleague and rival Ender Wiggin, Bean has been chosen to enroll in Battle School. And like Ender, Bean will be called upon to perform an extraordinary service. A parallel novel to the extraordinary *Ender's Game*.

"An exceptional work."—*School Library Journal*

H. M. Hoover

ORVIS

An American Booksellers
"Pick of the Lists"

Parents Choice Children's Media
Award for Literature

When Toby stumbles upon an abandoned robot named Orvis, she knows exactly how he feels. No one wants her either. With Orvis and her only friend Thaddeus—another lonely castoff—Toby sets off across the vast Empty in search of sanctuary.

"A first-rate adventure."—*Parents Choice*

ANOTHER HEAVEN, ANOTHER EARTH

An American Library Association
"101 Best of the Best Books in the Past 25 Years"

"Superb!"—*The Times Educational Supplement*

Only a handful of residents remain on Xilan from the original crew that colonized the planet centuries before. Including Gareth. When a rescue mission arrives from Earth, however, Gareth must make a difficult decision: accept their help and abandon the only past she has ever known . . . or cling to the past and risk extinction.

"A real blockbuster of a novel. As readable as it is wise."
—*The Junior Bookshelf*

Roderick MacLeish

PRINCE OMBRA

"Reminiscent of Bradbury's *Something Wicked This Way Comes*."
—*Publishers Weekly*

"Highly recommended."—*Library Journal*

"Whirls the reader along."—*Chicago Sun Times*

Bentley has secret powers. And he's going to need them. Bentley is a hero—the thousand and first to be exact—in a long line of heroes that has stretched all the way back to antiquity. Heroes like Arthur and Hercules. And now: Bentley. One day when Bentley is grown he will be that hero. What Bentley doesn't know is that his "one day" is today.

Caroline Stevermer

A COLLEGE OF MAGICS

"Strikingly set, pleasingly peopled, and cleverly plotted."
—*Kirkus Reviews* (pointer)

"Delightful!"—*The Washington Post*

Teenager Faris Nallaneen—heir to the dukedom of Galazon—is shunted off to Greenlaw College so that her evil uncle can lay claim to her inheritance. But Greenlaw is not just any school as Faris—and her uncle—will soon discover.

Joan Aiken

THE WHISPERING MOUNTAIN

Winner of the Guardian Prize for Fiction

"An enchanting, original story."
—*The Times* of London

In an effort to recover the magical Harp of Teirtu, Owen and his friend Arabis are plunged into a hair-raising adventure of intrigue, kidnapping, exotic underground worlds, savage beasts . . . even murder.

THE SHADOW GUESTS

"Writing seems to be as natural to Joan Aiken as breathing; her imagination is as untrammeled as ever, the precise construction of the astonishing plot lends conviction, and her style is as witty and sparkling with images."
—*The Horn Book*

After the mysterious disappearance of both his mother and older brother, Cosmo is sent away to live with his eccentric mathematician aunt. But things take a weird twist when Cosmo is visited by ghosts from the past. Ghosts who claim to need his help fighting an ancient deadly curse!

THE COCKATRICE BOYS
Illustrated by Gris Grimley

VOYA "Outstanding Science Fiction, Fantasy & Horror Books of the Year"

A plague of monsters has invaded England and Dakin and Sauna come to the rescue! A rollicking comic masterpiece.

Patricia C. Wrede

MAIRELON THE MAGICIAN

"Delightful . . . Wrede's confection will charm readers."
—*Publishers Weekly*

"A wonderful fantasy/mystery. Highly recommended."
—*VOYA*

When street urchin Kim is caught in the act stealing, her accuser surprises her by suggesting she become his apprentice. An apprentice to a magician!

THE MAGICIAN'S WARD

"A sure bet for fans of Philip Pullman's *Ruby in the Smoke* series."
—*VOYA*

Several wizards of Kim's acquaintance have mysteriously disappeared. And it's up to Kim to find out why.

Isobelle Carmody

OBERNEWTYN

in The Obernewtyn Chronicles

...or work of fantastic imagination."
—Lloyd Alexander

...lti-talented girl, her interesting friends,
...acters with minds of their own—this book
is a dream date for me."
—Tamora Pierce

...e freedom is—like so much else after the
...Great White—a memory. Feared because of
...tal powers, she and others like her are hunted

Tanith Lee

RED UNICORN

"Lavish, whimsical dreamscapes reminiscent of Lewis Carroll.
Lee's charming exuberance is everywhere in evidence,
no more so than in Tanaquil's familiar, a wonderfully

In this enchanting...is lured by a red
unicorn in...Tanakil, a
diabolical version of herself.